The Mirage

Nancy Rue

BETHANY HOUSE PUBLISHERS
MINNEAPOLIS, MINNESOTA 55438

A Focus on the Family book
Published by Bethany House Publishers
A Ministry of Bethany Fellowship International
11400 Hampshire Avenue South
Bloomington, Minnesota 55438
www.bethanyhouse.com

Printed in the United States of America by
Bethany Press International, Bloomington, Minnesota 55438

Library of Congress Cataloging-in-Publication Data

Rue, Nancy N.
    The mirage / Nancy Rue.
        p.   cm. — (Christian heritage series, the Santa Fe years)
Summary: In 1944 Santa Fe, Will Hutchinson must put his trust in God when his
Native American foster sister is accused of stealing by a Jewish shopkeeper who
seems to have some sinister secrets of his own.
    ISBN 1-56179-863-0
    [1. Prejudices—Fiction. 2. World War, 1939-1945—United States—Fiction.
3. Christian life—Fiction. 4. Mentally handicapped—Fiction. 5. Santa Fe
(N.M.)—Fiction.] I. Title.
    PZ7.R88515 Mg   2001
    [Fic]—dc21   00-012429

1 2 3 4 5 6 7 8 9 10 11 12 13 14 15 / 08 07 06 05 04 03 02 01

For Anne Wolf,

who makes God so real

There's More Adventure in the
CHRISTIAN HERITAGE SERIES!

The Salem Years, 1689–1691

The Rescue #1   *The Accused* #4
The Stowaway #2   *The Samaritan* #5
The Guardian #3   *The Secret* #6

The Williamsburg Years, 1780–1781

The Rebel #1   *The Prisoner* #4
The Thief #2   *The Invasion* #5
The Burden #3   *The Battle* #6

The Charleston Years, 1860–1861

The Misfit #1   *The Trap* #4
The Ally #2   *The Hostage* #5
The Threat #3   *The Escape* #6

The Chicago Years, 1928–1929

The Trick #1   *The Stunt* #4
The Chase #2   *The Caper* #5
The Capture #3   *The Pursuit* #6

The Santa Fe Years, 1944–1945

The Discovery #1   *The Mirage* #2

Chapter One

*W*ill Hutchinson waited until he heard his mom's bedroom door click shut before he turned on his flashlight under the covers. Then he listened to make sure she hadn't heard its snap. It was hard to put anything past Ingrid Hutchinson.

He opened the latest *TIME* magazine, June 1944, and gave one more hard listen toward the door. Mom was really strict about following the rules during blackouts.

I follow the rules, Will told himself as he flipped through the slick pages, looking for the article on spies that was advertised on the cover. *But I SERIOUSLY don't think any Japanese planes are going to see my flashlight beam through a window with a black shade on it—AND under my blanket!*

And definitely not any German planes, he added. What would Hitler's guys want in Santa Fe, New Mexico?

Will found the spy article and was about to pull the Tootsie Roll he'd been saving out of the pocket of his pajama top when he heard a rustle at the door. In one faster-than-electricity motion he snapped off the flashlight, shoved both it and the magazine under the pillow, and scrunched his eyes shut. He was even breathing sleep-heavy when the covers were whipped from over his head and a husky voice whispered, "You're not sleeping, you faker. Open your eyes."

Will did, to see his foster sister Fawn standing over him, arms folded across the front of her flowered summer bathrobe. It looked funny to him for a Native American Indian like Fawn to be dolled up in pink roses, but when his mother had taken her shopping at Sears to look at all the frilly stuff, they'd both squealed like the Japanese had just surrendered or something.

Fawn hiked the girly-looking bathrobe up to her knees like the tomboy she was and perched herself, uninvited, on the bed. Will didn't protest. For a girl, she was pretty okay, even if she was a year younger than he was, and besides, it had been just he and his mom for so long, it was kind of not bad having a sister—most of the time.

"You were reading with the flashlight again," she said.

Her small black eyes were sparkling, even in the almost-darkness of Will's room. There was a wide grin on her face, and with her full lips it made the bottom half of her face seem bigger than the upper half. Will's mom said that made her "engaging."

"So?" Will said.

"We're having a blackout. Nobody's supposed to have lights on."

"No kidding?" Will said. "Am I stupid?"

"What if the air raid warden catches you?"

"Since when does the air raid warden come up Canyon Road?"

"Oh, yeah." Fawn fished out a strand of her shoulder-length straight black hair and drew it under her nose like a moustache. "There could be 20 Nazis *living* on this road and nobody would even know it."

"Yeah," Will said. He tapped the magazine with his finger. "Or spies. This article I was reading says we oughta all be watching out for them and report them. Says they could be anywhere."

Fawn craned her neck to see the magazine. "What does a spy look like?"

"They don't *look* like spies," Will said in disgust. "If they did, they couldn't *be* spies because everybody would recognize them."

"Oh," Fawn said.

Will tried not to grin as she considered that. Fawn could get him into some wrestling holds he had to beg her to let him out of, but he could out-debate her any day of the week.

She nodded again at the magazine. "What else does it say?"

Will flipped a few more pages. "It says some of our army units discovered concentration camps in Poland."

"What's a concentration camp?"

"A place where Hitler's sending Jews because he doesn't like them."

"That couldn't be the truth," Fawn said.

"*TIME* magazine doesn't lie. The Germans put a couple of million Jewish people in these special gas chamber things and—" Will turned the page and stared at the photograph that stared back at him.

"And what?" Fawn said. "Let me see that."

Before Will could stop her, she grabbed the magazine out of his hand and scanned the picture. He saw the same horror in her black eyes that he knew was in his own blue ones.

"These are dead bodies, Will," she said.

"Yeah," Will said. "It says there that they put them in these gas chamber things and—" He nodded toward the picture. "You know."

Fawn thrust the *TIME* back at Will. "Isn't there anything happy in there?" she said. "Find something about the Signal Corps."

That was the branch her father was in in the war, and it was on the move so much, Fawn and her mother hardly ever got a letter from him. Sometimes it was all Will could do not to say, *At least you GET letters. People keep saying MY father's a Japanese prisoner of war. We NEVER get a letter.*

Of course, as long as they didn't get a telegram telling them Rudy Hutchinson was dead, Will could still hope, and he did—with all the hope-in-God he could muster. Still, though, if a person were realistic—

"Well, is there anything about the Signal Corps?" Fawn said.

Will scanned the table of contents and shook his head. "Nope," he said. "There's hardly ever anything about that—or the Special Branch either."

"Is that the thing your Uncle Al's in?"

"Yeah. It's not realistic to think they'd talk about that in here, though—'cause that's all secret stuff."

Fawn made herself comfortable on Will's bed and puckered her brow at him. "What's 'realistic' anyway?"

"You know, like when something makes sense, like you could actually expect it to happen."

"Give me an example."

"It's realistic to say Mom'll make us help her unpack tomorrow. It's *not* realistic to say that—okay, that you and I are blood brother and sister."

Fawn's brow puckered harder than ever. "Then I don't think I like realistic that much."

"That doesn't mean I don't like having you live here," he said quickly. There was something about the way her eyebrows were knitting tighter and tighter that was making this not as much fun as usual. "What I mean is—"

He was about to go on when he heard a noise outside. Fawn cocked her head toward the black window shade.

"Is that a car?" she said.

"It better not be. Nobody's supposed to be out driving around during a blackout."

They both leapt to the window, and Will pulled the black shade out just far enough for them each to get an eye to the crack. Blackout or no blackout, there was a car down there all right. Its lights were off, but Will could distinguish its bulky shape in the pitch-darkness, creeping slowly past the house.

"Is it coming or going?" Fawn whispered.

Will couldn't tell. The back looked exactly like the front.

Fawn nudged him in the side with her elbow. "Do you think it's a spy?"

"No, silly."

"How come? You said you didn't know what a spy looked like."

"I just know that isn't one," Will said. "It isn't realistic."

They watched the car round the bend in Canyon Road, and Fawn left the window.

"You sure use that word a lot," she said.

Will was still squinting out into the darkness. The driver probably wasn't a spy, but why *was* he cruising around during a blackout—and stopping in front of *their* house?

Hardly anybody even knows we live here yet, Will thought. They'd only moved in two days ago. They were still living out of boxes, for Pete's sake.

"Hey," Fawn said from the bed. "Why don't they put some *interesting* news in here? You could write better stuff than this."

"Huh?" Will said.

She was rifling restlessly through the *TIME*. "You keep that war scrapbook and write stuff in it all the time," she said. "That's more interesting to look at than this." She tossed the magazine onto the bedspread. "You know what? You oughta make your own magazine."

"Come on, be—"

"If you say 'realistic,' I'm gonna jump you."

"I'm ready for ya," Will said. He wiggled his fingers toward her. "Come on, try it."

"Nah—I gotta take you by surprise these days," she said. "You're getting too tough—I used to be able to pin you down whenever I wanted."

"You really think we could make our own magazine?"

"Not 'we'—'you,'" she said. "I can't spell worth a hoot."

"You wouldn't have to actually write," Will said. "But you could help get the facts and stuff."

"And pictures! I could use Mama Hutchie's camera and take pictures." She frowned at the magazine. "Not like the ones they have in there, but—"

Will put up his hand and shook his head sagely. "Forget it. It's not realistic. How would we get it printed up? And who would even buy it?"

Fawn scowled. "It's not as much fun since you got the realistics," she said.

Will shrugged and shoved the magazine under his bed where he would put his scrapbook as soon as he unpacked it. Fun or not, everything in *that* was for real, and that was just the way it was now.

"Is getting a bowl of cereal realistic?" she said.

"I guess so," he said. "As long as we don't turn on any lights."

"And as long as we can find some bowls."

They couldn't in the first three packing crates they looked in. They ended up eating cornflakes dry out of the box.

Mom didn't start unpacking the kitchen stuff until the next morning. Up until the week before she'd been working as a teacher, but now that school was out for the summer, she was ready to put that new house to rights. Anything she wasn't going to use for a while she sent up to the attic by Will and Fawn. There seemed to be a lot she wasn't going to use; by ten o'clock they were already dragging their feet and had little beads of sweat on their upper lips.

"Mama Hutchie!" Fawn wailed. "Can't we take a break?"

Will's mother poked her head out through the rounded archway to the kitchen and tucked a loose strand of her on-the-brown-side-of-blonde hair back into the braid she wore folded up at the nape of her neck. She had been working since before the sun came up, but her face wasn't even flushed yet. Although she and Will looked a lot alike, *un*like skinny, gangly Will, she was sturdy and never wasted energy on even thinking about getting tired. She surveyed them both with laughing eyes. Ingrid Hutchinson seldom smiled, but her eyes grinned most of the time.

"Ten minutes," she said. "And then back to work. We can't live out of boxes forever, and we've got a Victory Garden to start. I've got hoes for both of you."

Fawn wrinkled her nose. "I'd rather cart boxes."

"I thought so." Mom wrinkled her nose back, eyes still shiny. Will could always read her mood, and today it was especially clear: She liked being Fawn's substitute mom while Fawn's own mother, Frog Woman, was away in Arizona getting cured of a disease in her eyes. Will also knew his mom meant business, and he gave Fawn a poke.

"Come on. I got some gum—Juicy Fruit," he said. "We'll take one more load, and we can chew it up there."

"Please do," Mom said. "Spare me that disgusting aroma."

"She doesn't like the way Juicy Fruit smells," Will said as they hauled two more boxes up to the second floor and then up the narrow staircase to the attic. "She's mostly pretty swell, but one thing she hates is Juicy Fruit."

"What else does she hate?"

Will had to think about that. His mother didn't talk that much about hating things. She mostly talked about stuff she liked.

"She hates people being dishonest," Will said finally. "You know, like if they steal or lie or something."

"I don't ever do that," Fawn said. "So I got nothing to worry about."

"Except taking more than 10 minutes to rest."

But below Will heard the phone ring faintly, and he figured they had at least *12* minutes. Mom liked to talk on the phone. It got lonely for her without Dad—

He dug the last two sticks of Juicy Fruit out of the pocket of his dungarees and handed one to Fawn. She stuffed it hungrily into her mouth and chewed contentedly as she looked around the attic. "I like it up here," she said.

"It's okay, I guess," Will said. He added their last two boxes to the stack. "We better enjoy it now before she fills it up."

Fawn was already prowling around the room with its slanted ceiling, poking her finger into knot holes and jumping on the squeakier boards. Will sat on the floor by the one window and felt the dry early-summer air. It wasn't New-Mexico hot yet at the end of May, and the air was still crisp enough to cool the back of his neck.

"I got a question," Fawn said. "How come there's a window on the front of the house on the outside up here, but you can't see it from in here?"

Will tilted his head. "I don't know. It's a fake window or something."

"But why?"

He shrugged. She was getting to be as much of an arguer as he was, and right now all he wanted to do was chew lazily at his Juicy Fruit and—do nothing. That was what summer was for, right?

"Hello!" Fawn said suddenly. She was on her hands and knees in the middle of the attic, looking at the floor.

"What?" he said.

"I found a ring." Fawn lifted it up with a finger, and a square piece of the floor came up with it. "It was attached to this lid."

Will scrambled up and joined her. The "lid" she'd opened revealed a snug compartment in the attic floor. Inside was a wooden box.

"Treasure!" Fawn said. "Just like in that movie we saw!"

They both grabbed it and pulled it out together. Fawn blew on the top, sending dust flying right at Will. As he snorted the dust out of his nose, she lifted its hinged lid—and her shoulders sagged.

"This isn't treasure," she said, as if some vow made to her had just been grossly violated. "It's just a bunch of papers."

"Yeah, but they might be war bonds or something," Will said. "Let me see."

Fawn plunked a bundle of envelopes into his hand in disgust. They were tied together with a blue ribbon as if someone had been carefully wrapping a package. Will didn't undo it but nudged one of the envelopes out and pulled a folded piece of paper from it.

"Hey," Fawn said, eyes suddenly sparking to life again, "what if there's a treasure map in there?"

"Would you be realistic?" Will said. He frowned at the paper. "It's just a letter—and it's in some kinda foreign language."

"Spanish?"

"No—something else." He frowned at it. "It's to somebody named Joanna, but that's all I can tell."

"Hey, you two—that's the longest ten minutes in the history of time," Mom called from below.

Fawn dropped the box back into its compartment and replaced the piece of floorboard. "I'm hiding these again."

"What for?"

" 'Cause—I like having stuff. I don't have that much stuff."

Mom met them at the bottom of the stairs with two boxes.

"Not more stuff to go up to the attic!" Fawn said.

"No," Mom said. "I'm sending you out of here with these. They're your old children's books, Will. I want you to take them to the Opportunity School."

"I never heard of that school," Fawn said.

"Some Catholic Sisters started it a few years ago," Mom said. "It's all run on donations, so I thought they could use these."

"Who was on the phone?" Fawn said.

Mom's lips twitched. "NOT that it's necessarily any of your business, but it was Pastor Bud. He was reminding Will about getting together with him Thursday."

"Can I go?" Fawn said.

"No," Will said. "It's boys only."

"No fair!"

"Put your lower lip away, Fawn," Mom said. "You and I are going on our own outing Thursday. Picnic up at the Cross of the Martyrs. I haven't hiked in ages; you're just the person to escort me."

"Yeah! Can we have marzipan—I love your marzipan—and we'll go—"

"We'll do it all if you get this errand done. Will—let me give you directions—"

And Will and Fawn were off, each with a box, toward the center of Santa Fe.

It wasn't far to where Mom said the school was. Nothing was very far from anything else in the quiet, sleepy town, and Will didn't mind walking that much. There was plenty of shade from the cottonwoods, and their leaves sounded like clapping as they touched each other.

Besides, it was fun walking by the Palace of the Governors, even though that meant going the long way, carrying boxes of books, no less. But he never got tired of looking at the Indian jewelry that was spread out on blankets by the Native women on the portal of the Palace. It was all handmade from silver and turquoise, and it shone even in the shade.

Fawn usually turned her nose up at all that and waited at the Woolworth's window on the other side of the Plaza where she could see the "white kids' toys." Although she'd been born and mostly raised on the San Ildefonso Pueblo, she wanted to be like a white girl. "Indian stuff" didn't interest her.

When they got to the end of San Francisco Street, she jerked her dark head toward the pink limestone walls of the St. Francis Cathedral across from them. "Mama Hutchie said the school was back there."

Will started to follow her across the intersection when something caught his eye to their left. He stiffened when he saw what it was.

"What's wrong?" Fawn said.

Will turned straight toward St. Francis. "Don't look behind you."

Of course, she immediately stopped and twisted her head around, and Will had to shove her toward the crossing at Cathedral Place.

"What's back there?" she said.

"Just keep going. It's Luis and them."

"So?" Fawn said. "Why are we scared of them?"

"We're not scared, exactly," Will said, trying to keep his eyes straight ahead. "But Luis never got back at me for making our team look stupid over the war stamp contest—and for letting them tell everybody I was rich when I wasn't." He swallowed hard. "Luis just doesn't like anybody making him look like a fool."

"He already IS one," Fawn said, and she planted her feet on the curb. "Bring 'em on."

"Forget it," Will said.

"No. We don't gotta run from anybody, Will. We're Hutchinsons."

Fawn dropped her box of books on the sidewalk and turned

toward the three Hispanic boys who were now only half a block away on San Francisco Street.

"Come on, Fawn," Will said, shifting his own box, which was getting heavier by the second. "We gotta get this stuff to the school—"

But it was as if he weren't even speaking. Fawn already had her fists clenched and her eyes narrowed above her straight Indian nose.

All that's missing is the war paint, Will thought. He groaned half out loud and once more shoved at her with his box.

"Be realistic, Fawn," he hissed at the back of her neck. "There's three of them and only two of us. Forget about it."

Whether she would have or not, he didn't have a chance to find out—because just then the three boys sprang into a run straight toward them. The tallest one, the one with the raggediest clothes and the meanest eyes, took the lead and reached the corner before Will could even think about moving.

Fawn stepped directly into his path, blocking his way to Will. "Where do you think *you're* goin', Luis?" she said.

Luis didn't answer. He just threw out his arm and slammed it against Fawn. She fell to the ground like a sack of dirt.

✝ ⬦ ✝

Chapter Two

*F*awn set up a holler that stopped the mourning doves in mid-flutter. It didn't stop Luis. The Spanish-American boy was as tall as Will and a lot sturdier, and he merely stepped over Fawn and came right at Will.

Will took a step backward and put his box between them, his mind racing. "So now you're picking on little girls, huh, Luis?" he said. "Too bad you had to sink to that."

Luis didn't answer. The fact that his two friends, Rafael and Pablo, had now joined him to surround Will made that entirely unnecessary. Pablo, in his holey overalls, was little and pale, and blue-eyed Rafael with the tattered plaid shirt that hung open wasn't the smartest kid around, but the three of them together were more than Will wanted to take on.

Besides, this whole thing was a surprise. Sure they were mad because he'd lied to them—but was that grounds for all this shoving around?

On the fringe of his vision Will could see Fawn scrambling to get up. But at Luis's nod, Rafael planted a foot in the middle of her back. Will shifted his eyes around, hoping to see a policeman, a passing store clerk, even an old lady shopping for tamales who might break this thing up, but the street was in its usual sleepy state. At the moment, there wasn't another person in sight.

With Luis now up in his face, Will knew he couldn't wait around for help to show up. Luis had never hit him—but suddenly the possibility was there in his mean, dark eyes, and in the sullen way his mouth hung partway open. Whatever it was that was bugging Luis, Will didn't want to know about it, but he said anyway, "So whatta ya want? We don't have a lot of time."

"I got time," Luis said.

Rafael reached around Luis to give Pablo a poke. Those two nudged each other practically every time Luis spoke. It was a good thing Luis seldom said much or they'd both be black and blue. But that was the worst they'd ever done as far as Will knew. Those two were clowns as far as he was concerned. But Luis—

"Time for what?" Will said.

"To get you," Luis said.

"Why? I already said I was sorry about what happened with the war stamps and the lying and stuff. I already made up for that. Besides, that was weeks ago."

Luis slid his eyes toward Rafael. Obviously he wanted to say something that took more than three words. He usually had Rafael say the longer stuff.

"You might *think* you made up for it," Rafael said, practically licking his chops. "But *we* don't think so. You made us look real bad. Luis—he don't forget that."

Luis squinted his eyes so hard they nearly disappeared into his dark face. He ignored the squawking that was still coming from the sidewalk below them and lifted his upper lip to sneer at Will. "I will get you, An-glow," he said.

Will hoped Luis didn't see his Adam's apple as he swallowed the fear-lump in his throat. He looked down at Fawn, who had managed to turn over onto her back and was about to sink her teeth into Rafael's ankle. It gave Will a spurt of courage.

"So go ahead, then," he said. "Sock me in the nose."

Luis peered at him suspiciously. Just as Will had hoped, Fawn chose that moment to chomp into Rafael's flesh. He yelped like a puppy and hopped on one foot, clutching the other one between his hands. Luis whipped around, just in time for Fawn to grab him around both legs and topple him to the ground.

"Grab your box and run, Fawn!" Will shouted.

Fawn did, but not before she stuck out her foot and tripped Pablo and sent him, too, sprawling to the sidewalk. She and Will were across the street and disappearing into the shadows of St. Francis Cathedral before any of them recovered. But as they dashed past the steps Will heard Luis yell, "I WILL get you, An-glow—and HER, too!"

"Not in a thousand years," Fawn said when they'd rounded the corner of the cathedral and could stop to catch their breath. Will was getting to be a better runner after all these months of tearing around with, and being chased by, Fawn. But doing it while carrying a box of books was another matter. He was gasping for air—and even Fawn was breathing harder than usual.

"They're just talking big," he managed to say.

"I hope not. I'd *like* to have an excuse to wrestle that Luis boy. I'd take him, you know."

Will was sure she could, but that wasn't the point. The point was to stay OUT of trouble altogether. After the things that had happened in the spring, neither one of them could afford to mess up again. They'd only recently won back Mom's trust, and that was something Will didn't want to lose again.

"Come on," he said quickly. "We can't do it carrying all this stuff. We were about to have Little Golden Books scattered all over San Francisco Street as it was."

Just as Mom had told them, there were several old adobe buildings behind the cathedral. But they looked more like some chicken houses and a stable and a storage room than a school, although they had indented windows through which Will could see girls working at hand looms and boys bending over saws.

There were some kids about 12 years old digging holes in front of one of the buildings, and they all looked up and gaped, open-mouthed, at Will and Fawn as they passed. There was something funny about the way they blinked at Will, as if they couldn't decide if he were boy or beast.

"Don't they know it's rude to stare?" Fawn whispered to Will as they hurried on toward the main building.

"Since when are you an expert on manners?" he whispered back. But he was glad he wasn't the only one who'd noticed the kids were—different.

Soon after they knocked on the first door, a lady with a face that was one big smile opened it for them and bobbed her head at them about 30 times before she even spoke. She was wearing the long black dress and veil of a nun, her pink face puffing out from the white wimple as if it had been squeezed into it.

"Why, hello, my dears, my dears!" she said. "Come in, come in— mercy, what do you have here? What do you have?"

Will opened his mouth to answer her, but she bubbled on before he could get a word out.

"I'm Sister Miriam George, Miriam George. And who would you be? And what do you have here—what do you have?"

"We're—"

"Come in first, come in—it's too hot out there—you need some lemonade. The girls just made some, just made some. Now, what is it you've brought?"

"Ourmomsentuswithbooksforyou."

Will took a breath as he watched the Sister work that out. Then her face returned to its pink smile, and she began to bob again. "Books for us—books for us—how lovely, my dears—how lovely! Then you absolutely *must* have lemonade. Must have it."

She swept them with her through the building, flapping her black-clad arms out like wings as she gestured toward "the main classroom, main classroom—the work room for crafts, 1,000 potholders a year, 1,000 a year—and the kitchen, the kitchen, we're so proud of the kitchen—"

"How come she says everything twice?" Fawn whispered to Will.

"You got me," Will whispered back. "I wanna know when we get to put these boxes down."

Sister Miriam George took care of that at the door to "the library, the library" and then continued flapping them on toward the kitchen. All along the way, faces poked out of doorways, all with some version of the staring Will and Fawn had received outside. A few of them spoke, but Will couldn't understand a thing they were saying.

They must be foreigners, Will thought. But Santa Fe was mostly Spanish and some American Indian and a handful of Anglos like himself. He hadn't known there to be any other nationalities represented, and that sure wasn't Spanish or Tewa they were speaking.

"What if they're spies?" Fawn whispered.

"Be realistic," Will whispered back.

In the big sunny kitchen, three girls served them lemonade in jelly jars and then ran, giggling, back behind their counters. They were older than Fawn but they acted three years younger. It was enough to make Will sniff at the lemonade before he took the first sip. He was surprised at how good it was, and he gulped it down while the Sister continued to bob and tell them about the Opportunity School.

"I can't take the credit, can't take it," she said. "God asked Sister Mary Harold and me to found it together when we were teaching at the Cathedral school." She shook her wimpled head. "So many mentally deficient children in our classroom and no time to help them— no time at all. Come, let me show you the workshop—"

"What's 'mentally deficient'?" Fawn said as they followed her out of that building and into another.

"Like they can't think too good," Will said. "Oh—that must be why they sound like they're foreigners. They can't talk too good either."

Fawn's eyes widened, and she drew closer to Will. "You mean, they're nuts?"

"No! But they're probably not all that smart." He and Fawn followed Sister Miriam George into the building that looked like a chicken house on the outside. "I think there's something kind of wrong with them," he added.

The door closed behind them, and with a flourish Sister Miriam presented a workshop where boys were at workbenches, some of them sawing intently at wood, others carving with smaller tools, and one even working a lathe. Will could feel his own eyes widening when he saw that the boy had only one arm.

"They're making a theater for our annual puppet show—yes, puppet show," Sister Miriam George said proudly. "The puppets themselves will be made out of papier-mâché—that's done in the crafts room. Have I shown you the crafts room?"

Will shook his head. Fawn pointed to the one-armed boy. "How can he do that?" she said. "Aren't you afraid he's going to cut the other arm off?"

Will groaned inwardly.

"No, no," Sister Miriam George said. "He's been given individual attention, just like all our students, mentally and physically handicapped alike—mentally and physically. It takes endless repetition and perseverance—and the grace of God, of course. The grace of God, yes. It's all a miracle."

Will could see Fawn winding up to ask what perseverance was, but Sister Miriam George was already moving on. "I must show you the crafts room—that's my particular pride and joy, yes . . ."

"Pride and joy," Will muttered along with her.

The Sister chattered on as she walked, explaining how many people gave money to support the school, and how each child got a hot lunch every day and books and tuition and the use of all the tools and materials in handcrafts and woodwork and weaving—Catholic and non-Catholic students alike.

"God loves all His children," she told them as she turned a corner in the hallway. "All His children—"

Will didn't hear the rest of what she said, because as he turned the corner himself a door to his left opened, and something big and soft and thick hit him in the side of the head and knocked him against the opposite wall. More big, soft, thick things piled on him until he thought he was going to suffocate.

He tried to yell "Hey!" but "Meh!" was all that came out. It felt like someone was stuffing cotton into his mouth.

He heard a muffled "Mercy, mercy!" coming from Sister Miriam George and a mishmash of confusion before somebody finally dug a hole big enough for Will to see through. A face poked in at him, all cheeks and eyes and teeth. *"Guten Tag!"* it said.

"What?" Will said through the hole.

"Abe—speak English, please. English!" said Sister Miriam George.

Could we work on his language skills later? Will thought furiously. *I'd like to get out from under—whatever this is!*

"Whatever it was" turned out to be a pile of pillows in brilliant colors. Fawn pulled them off one by one, grinning the entire time. As soon as he got his feet free, Will pulled himself up and glared at her.

"I didn't do it!" she said. "He did."

She pointed to the owner of the cheeks and eyes and teeth. They belonged to a somewhat lumpy-looking boy with butter-blond hair and a round face of flaming skin and hazel eyes that looked as big as silver dollars. He was still smiling at Will, revealing a set of gigantic white teeth. He smiled so big he seemed to have more of them than the average person. Will could practically see his molars.

"Good morning!" the boy said. His voice was heavy and dull and didn't match the pure excitement he was exhibiting otherwise as he bounced and jiggled. *He either thinks I'm President Roosevelt,* Will thought, *or he has to go to the bathroom.*

"This is Abe," Sister Miriam George said. "Abe, meet—" She stopped and looked surprised. "I don't even know your names yet!"

Not that you ever gave us a chance to say them, Will thought as

Fawn introduced them. He glowered at the mound of pillows that Abe was attempting to load into his arms again. There was some sort of gurgling sound coming out of the boy's mouth. It took Will a minute to realize he was giggling. The more pillows he lost control of, the more he gurgled.

It seemed out of place, coming from a boy who was at least two heads taller even than Will. From the size of him, Will decided he should have been at least 15, and yet he acted as if he were about eight.

"Abe," Sister Miriam George said, "this is Will Hutchinson. Introduce yourself now, introduce yourself. And in English, in English."

Abe dropped the pillows and stuck out a meaty hand and grabbed Will's, shaking it with enthusiasm. "I'm Abe—" He finished with Something or Other That Sounded Like It Started With an F.

"Nice to meet you," Will mumbled, and then glanced around for the nearest exit.

Abe looked at Sister Miriam George, who bobbed her head. "Nicely done, Abe," she said. "Nicely done."

The boy bobbed back, and giggled, and gurgled. Then, as if he'd just had a brilliant idea, he bounded back to the pile of pillows, selected a bright turquoise one, and bounded back to Will and thrust it at him. This time it missed his face and bounced against his chest.

"How generous of you, Abe!" the Sister said. "How generous. He wants you to have that, Will. He made it himself. He makes rugs, too."

Abe nodded excitedly and started toward the door.

Convinced the boy was going to fetch a handmade carpet and make Will take *that* home as well, Will jerked his head at Fawn and said, "We gotta go."

"Abe, it's time for you to go home, too, or you'll be in trouble," Sister Miriam George said. "Hurry now."

Will pushed Fawn toward the front door while Abe bumbled out the back.

"Please come back, come back again," Sister Miriam George said to them. "Oh—don't forget your pillow."

Will took the somewhat lopsided cushion and stuffed it under his arm as he followed Fawn out the door at an almost-run.

"What am I gonna do with this?" he said when they were out of Sister Miriam George's earshot.

Fawn stopped at the doorway that led outside. "Put it over our heads," she said. "It's pouring down rain."

In true New Mexico fashion, the day had turned from brilliant blue to daytime-black in the short time they'd been inside, and the sky had opened up to dump its contents in big, heavy drops.

They stood there for at least 10 minutes, waiting for it to slow down as it almost always did. But the more the dry, hard ground sucked it up, the harder it seemed to fall.

"We gotta get out of here before that nun makes us spend the night or something," Will said.

"Then run!" Fawn said, and she took off between the school buildings toward the cathedral.

Will set out after her, trying to keep dry under the pillow. They kept on down Cathedral Place and around the corner to Water Street, but before they reached Santa Fe Trail, the pillow was heavy with rain water and even Fawn was slowing down.

"In here!" she called over her shoulder and darted into the doorway of one of the shops.

By the time Will caught up with her, she had already gone inside. Her face crumpled into laughter when he followed her in and shut the door behind him.

"What's so funny?" Will said.

But before she could answer, the door jangled behind him, and the sound of the rain grew louder as it opened. Fawn's eyes shifted toward it and went hard. Will turned to see, and felt his own gaze go stiff.

Standing behind them were Pablo, Rafael, and, of course—Luis.

✝-✦-✝

Chapter Three

*W*ill let the pillow drop with a wet thud to the floor. Fawn stepped in front of him, little fists already doubled.

Luis, however, didn't have his ready for the first punch. In fact, he looked a little dazed, as if spotting Will and Fawn going into the curio shop were an unexpected stroke of luck. A bright thought came into Will's head: If the three Hispanic boys were surprised, that probably meant they didn't have a plan.

But Will himself wasn't going to be without one. Before Luis could make a move toward Fawn—or she could direct her teeth toward his skin—Will scooped up the soaking-wet pillow and thrust it over Fawn's head, straight into Luis's face.

At least, that was where it was *meant* to go. Instead, it grazed Rafael's shoulder, veered off, and landed on a shelf cluttered with tacky Indian dolls and cheap jewelry. The pieces fell like dominos and clattered in a shower to the floor.

"Ach!" said a gruff voice from somewhere behind them. "What you kids are doing?"

For a few seconds everybody froze, even Luis. It wasn't until they all heard footsteps scuffling angrily toward them that the confusion began. Fawn hit the floor to avoid being slugged by Luis and took that opportunity to take a bite out of Pablo's ankle. Luis leaned down to get her, but Will snatched up the pillow and smacked him in the back of the head with it. Rafael tried to come to the rescue, but he skidded on a doll and landed with his rear end on Luis.

They were all in a hopeless pile when a short man wearing wire-rimmed glasses careened into the aisle and said, "Stop it NOW!"

Will hardly dared look up, and when he did, he saw a long nose, a straight line of a mouth, and a pair of the biggest ears he'd ever seen except on a burro. It was all attached to an oblong head that looked as if it had been stretched into that shape by some unseen hand. The man's gray hair had been cut very short except for one shock that fell over his forehead, making his ears look even larger.

Luis and company didn't take the time to check out the shop-keeper's appearance. They untangled themselves from Fawn and Will and headed for the door, even as the man shouted, "Stop! Stop at once, I say!"

The door jangled shut behind them, and Fawn tried to lunge for it, too, but the big-eared man snatched at her arm and picked her up so that she was suddenly right up against him. She tried to pull away, her eyes blazing, but he held on for another pull. This time she wriggled from his grasp and although he missed catching her again, his fingers snagged onto the pocket of her shorts. A miniature Indian doll fell from it and hit the floor, joining the rest of the scattered merchandise.

"Ach!" the man cried out. "What that was doing in your pocket, eh?"

Fawn got to her feet and stared at it, shaking her head.

"You don't know? Of course you know!" The man's voice thundered—over the rain, over the pounding of Will's pulse in his ears. "You were trying to steal from me!"

"No!" Fawn said. Her dark eyes were startled. "I didn't take that!"

"And what else is in your pocket?"

The man pointed to an obvious bulge in Fawn's shorts. Will, too, stared at it, and then at Fawn. He had never seen her look helpless, but just then she might just as well have been standing blindfolded before a firing squad.

"What is that? Let me see it!" the shopkeeper said. "Take it out!"

The man's voice had reached a dangerous pitch. Fawn gave Will a begging look, but he couldn't think of even a single argument.

"Take it out!" the man cried again, and then made a move as if to remove the object from Fawn's pocket himself.

She dodged his grasp and stuck her hand in. A new terror flickered through her eyes, and she pulled out a large decorative pin, made from obviously cheap metal with a glob of turquoise glued to it.

"My jewelry!" the man shouted, so loudly that strings of Indian beads jiggled nervously on their rack. "You tried to steal my jewelry—and my dolls!"

"No, I didn't!" Fawn's lower lip was quivering. "Will—tell him I didn't."

Will fumbled for an answer. "She didn't, Mister," he said. "There's dolls and jewelry and stuff all over the floor. Some of it just got caught in there."

Fawn was nodding her head so hard, she could have out-bobbed Sister Miriam, but the shopkeeper was shaking his just as intently.

"These things will not 'get caught' so deep in a pocket," he said. He brought a dried-up finger close to Fawn's nose. "You—stole!"

"Come on, Mister," Will said. "That's not realistic. Fawn's an Indian herself—she could *make* better stuff than this. Why would she want yours?"

"Who knows?" the man thundered. "Why do these Indians do anything they do, eh? Because—they are—evil!"

If anything was "evil" it was the look in the man's eyes as he drilled them into Fawn. She stepped back and leaned against Will. Feisty, nobody-can-take-me Fawn was trembling like a spooked jackrabbit.

"You don't know what you're talking about—sir!" Will cried.

He knew his mother would want that "sir" thrown in there, but he sure didn't feel like being polite. He *felt* like snatching the old man's glasses off and crushing them under his heel. As it was, he grabbed Fawn's wrist and pulled her toward the door.

"I'm sorry your stuff got knocked over," he said, "and I'll pay for anything that got broken, but don't accuse her of stealing."

With a swiftness Will didn't expect of him, the old man stepped between the kids and the door and, with a deft twist of his wrist, locked it.

"I have ALREADY accused her," he said, eyes still glinting. "And now I am going to call the police, who will call her parents and yours, AFTER they arrest you—"

Will and Fawn looked at each other, and Will was sure his eyes were as terrified as the ones that looked back at him.

"Don't bother trying to run," the man called over his shoulder as he hurried toward the phone behind the counter. "You won't get away with it."

They didn't "bother." Fawn sagged against Will, and they waited in silence for the shopkeeper to finish his phone call. By the time the door was unlocked and it jangled open again, Fawn was near tears and Will was ready to throw up. The store owner was standing over them, arms folded over his vest as if he had just captured an entire battalion of Japanese soldiers single-handedly, when the police officer came in.

"I didn't do it!" Fawn said.

The policeman, who had a pencil-thin black mustache and snapping black eyes to match, looked annoyed. He glanced only slightly at Fawn and Will and then directed his irritated gaze at the store owner.

"Again, Mr. Spitz?" he said.

"Ach, Perez!" Mr. Spitz said. "Why did they send *you*? I told them I didn't want you this time!"

"Doesn't matter what you 'want,' " Officer Perez said. "This is my beat. I take the calls here." He gave Fawn and Will another glance. "Are these the perpetrators?"

"I'm not a—I'm not one of those!" Fawn said. "And neither is Will!"

By now Will had found his own tongue. "Whatever a 'perpe-thinga-ma-jigger' is, we aren't that. I can explain everything. See—"

But Officer Perez shushed him with a wave of his hand and glared again at Mr. Spitz. "This is the third time this week you've called us for one of your suspected five-cent thefts, and the tenth time this month. Don't you think we have more important things to do?"

"What is more important than stopping this thievery? I caught them red-handed this time!"

"Did you see them take something off the shelf?"

"No—better. I found this, and this, in her pocket!"

Mr. Spitz held out the doll with the misshapen face and the pin with the glob of bad turquoise and nodded as if he had just secured Will and Fawn's imprisonment for life. Officer Perez squinted at it.

"This is what you're so worked up about?" he said.

"This is my livelihood!" Mr. Spitz said. His cloudy-gray eyes threatened to bulge out right through his glasses. "I have to sell this to support myself and my grandson. It is not bad enough I got high-falutin Indians telling me my merchandise is inferior—it is not bad enough we hardly got tourists this summer, only soldiers passing through to buy things—and now I got to put up with children robbing me blind, and police who won't do a thing about it!"

The man's face seemed to be getting longer and redder as he ranted. Even his large ears were the color of chili peppers.

Officer Perez stroked his thin mustache. "All right, all right," he said. "But why don't you just accept an apology from these two and let it go, Mr. Spitz? I'm sure it won't happen again, will it, kids?"

"It never happened in the first place!" Will said.

"And I am NOT apologizing for something I didn't even do!" Fawn stomped a foot for emphasis.

"I'm sick of the children coming in here, taking my things." Mr.

Spitz waved his arm, revealing a large, dark circle of perspiration in his armpit. "No, this is NOT the first time this happened, but it IS the first time I have caught one—and I am not letting go!"

With that he reached out and grabbed Fawn's arm. Before Officer Perez could even take a step, Fawn had snatched herself away and was threatening to direct her elbow at Mr. Spitz's belly.

"Whoa, there, missy," Officer Perez said. Firmly he steered her toward the doorway and nodded for Will to follow. "I'll take care of it, Mr. Spitz," he said over his shoulder. "Don't worry about it, all right?"

Will didn't like the sound of that, and he envisioned himself and Fawn in a dark cell with rats in it—

But once they were outside the shop, standing out of reach of the drips from the eaves which were the only remnant of the short thunderstorm, Officer Perez let go of Fawn's arm and shook his head.

"I'm sorry that happened, kids," he said. "Mr. Spitz has been convinced ever since he moved here a couple months ago that everybody is out to get him. People around here call him a cranky old Jew. Not a nice thing to say, I'll grant you that, but he almost asks for it."

"He didn't have to be cranky at me," Fawn said, glaring at the door. "I didn't do anything."

"You sure?"

"Yes!" they both said together.

Officer Perez gave Fawn's pocket a doubtful glance, but then he shook his head and gave a wave with his hand. "All right," he said. "But don't come back to this shop anytime soon. Do we agree?"

"Anytime *soon?*" Fawn said as the officer strolled away. "I'm *never* coming back here—*ever!*"

"Me neither," Will said. "Let's get outa here."

"And you know what else?" she said as she skipped to keep up with his long-legged, angry stride.

"What?"

"I betcha that Mr. Spitz is a spy."

"Oh, come on, Fawn," Will said. "He couldn't be a spy. He draws too much attention to himself."

"Maybe that's part of his act. Nobody would suspect him of being a spy because he doesn't act like one."

"We gotta be realistic, though," Will said.

"Here we go again."

"When we tell Mom about this, we better leave out the part about thinking Mr. Spitz is a spy. She'll think—"

"What do you mean 'when we tell Mom'?" Fawn stopped dead on the sidewalk and stood with her hands on her hips. "We can't tell her!"

"Why not?" Will said. "We didn't do anything wrong."

"But what if she thinks we did—or I did?"

"She wouldn't think that!"

"Yeah, but—just don't tell her, all right?"

"I'm through keepin' stuff from my mom," Will said. "She made me promise."

"That would count if we really had done something bad, or if that policeman had arrested us. But nothing happened, Will."

To his surprise, Fawn's eyes were starting to fill up with tears.

"Why are you cryin'?" he said.

"I'm not!" she said. She smeared at the corners of her eyes with her fingers. "Now listen to me—Mama Hutchie might change her mind about keeping me if she finds out there's been trouble *already*. Please, Will?"

Will had to hesitate. As much as he didn't want to keep any more secrets from his mother, he also didn't want her to have a change of heart about Fawn living with them. It was so much better since she came—so much less lonesome, with Dad gone—

"Just this once," he said. "And we gotta just avoid Luis and those guys—period."

"After we get back at them."

"No—no more getting back. That's my final deal."

Fawn frowned, but she nodded. "Okay—unless one of them starts something."

"That's why we're gonna stay away from them. I'm not kiddin', Fawn."

By now they were almost to the house. Fawn slowed her steps.

"I'm only doing this because I want to stay with you and Mama Hutchie," she said. "But just so you know—Luis shouldn't be allowed to just beat up on whoever he wants—especially you."

"Let it go," Will said.

Mom opened the front screen door just then. "Come in here and get changed, you two drowned rats," she said. "I'm taking you out to dinner—I still haven't unearthed the pots and pans."

"Plaza Restaurant?" they both said.

"Looks that way," Mom said.

That announcement erased everything else. As far as Will was concerned, the Plaza Restaurant was the only place to eat in town besides Ingrid Hutchinson's kitchen. Mom made the best good old American food on the planet, and her German desserts she'd learned from her German bakery-owner parents were to die for. But when it came to New Mexican food, nobody cooked it like the chefs at the Plaza.

It wasn't as ritzy as the name sounded, Will decided as Mom pulled the Hudson into a metered parking place beneath the neon sign that said HOME OF FINE FOOD. There were venetian blinds on the windows, and, as on most warm days, the front door was propped open in a neighborly way.

Inside were red leather booths and black tables, the ones against the wall bordered with a foot-high mirror that ran all around the room. Waitresses in ruffled aprons over their black skirts and white tops bustled across the black and white floor, their wide, white headbands darting like frisky dashes among the tables.

Mr. Razatos, the owner, stepped out from behind the huge arrangement of artificial flowers on the counter and straightened his bow tie as he greeted them.

"Mrs. Hutchinson!" he said warmly. "Table for three this evening?"

"Is our usual available?" Mom said.

Will pulled his eyes away from the clock that always fascinated him, the one with the neon letters around it saying TIME TO EAT, and looked toward the corner booth where he and Mom and Fawn always sat with whomever else they brought along.

Rats, he thought. There was already somebody there, a salt-and-pepper-haired man with his nose in today's *New Mexican*. *If he's just gonna sit there and read, why does he need our special table?*

Will was about to suggest that they ask him to move, but Mom was already moving, straight toward the booth. The man looked up in surprise when Mom leaned over him and said, "Judge Kohn? Ingrid Hutchinson. We met at Margetta Dietrich's about two months ago?"

"Of course!" The man's somewhat stern face broke into a smile and he stood up, letting the newspaper drop to the seat. "Will you join me?" he said.

"We thought you'd never ask," Mom said. "You don't mind a couple of rapscallions, do you?"

The judge extended his smile to Will and Fawn and ushered them both into the booth.

"This *is* our special table, you know," Fawn said to him.

"Oh, really?" the judge said. "How so?"

His very tiny bright blue eyes were twinkling—in a way that kind of reminded Will of his dad's. It was as if he were thinking about some joke, even when there wasn't one.

But he's a judge, Will thought. *Be realistic—he doesn't have time for jokes.*

"This is Fawn, Judge," Mom was saying. "You'll have to excuse her lack of tact—she likes to get right to the point."

"Girl after my own heart," Judge Kohn said. "And who is this serious young man?"

He was looking at Will, but Mom looked around the restaurant, her own eyes twinkling. "Where?" she said.

"He's not serious," Fawn said from over the top of her menu. "He's just realistic."

"Hush up, Fawn," Will said. He could feel his cheeks getting hot.

"Nothing wrong with being realistic," the judge said. "I'm something of a realist myself."

"I guess you would have to be in your line of work," Mom said.

"Actually I've found a sense of humor comes in handy more than a serious mind most of the time."

"Do you know any jokes?" Fawn said.

"Fawn, what are you having?" Mom said. "Don't wait until the waitress gets here to decide. The place closes at 10, you know."

Fawn happily perused the menu, and Will sneaked his eyes up over his at Judge Kohn. He was busy talking to Mom, which gave him a chance to take a complete inventory.

The judge was broad-shouldered and had a short, thick neck so that he reminded Will of a football player. A retired one, of course, because his face was cut into shallow crevices with age lines, and his graying hair, though wavy, was growing thin on top. *If I was accused of a crime*, Will thought, *I guess I'd want him for my judge.*

That afternoon's misadventure flickered through his mind, and he focused on the menu.

After everybody had ordered and the waitress had brought a plate of paper-thin blue corn tortillas for them to snack on, the judge folded his hands on the table and surveyed Fawn and Will as if they amused him terribly. Fawn, as usual, met that with suspicion.

"What?" she said. "Did I do something wrong?"

The judge chuckled. "Not that I know of. You're a spunky little thing, aren't you?"

"You hit that nail right on the head," Mom said. "I'm hard put to keep up with her."

"What kind of trouble are you two getting into to keep yourselves occupied this summer?" the judge said.

Will felt Fawn kick him under the table. He hoped his eyes weren't bulging out too far.

"No trouble," he managed to say. "In fact, we actually did a good deed today."

"I haven't even asked you—how did it go at the Opportunity School?" Mom said.

"Those kids are weird," Fawn said.

"Fawn!" Mom said.

"Now there's one of God's miracles, that school." The judge looked up at the ceiling fan as if he were seeing the past in it. "I remember in '39 when they started renovating those outbuildings—we all thought those two nuns were crazy."

"One of them still is," Fawn mumbled.

"How come everybody says it's a miracle?" Will said.

The judge chewed thoughtfully on a piece of tortilla. "They started with basically nothing but a desire to reach children who couldn't keep up in school. No money—no business plan. The whole thing's been built on faith and love and confidence in God, and it's maintained the same way."

"That nun—Sister Miriam George or something—she told us people gave donations," Will said.

"It costs $15 to sponsor a child," said the judge. "I sponsor several myself."

Will waited while the waitress put the plates of lamb garnished with wild horsemint and the bowls of bean soup in front of them, and then he said, "How is that a miracle, then? People give money for things all the time."

The judge's tiny blue eyes shone at Will. "You don't believe in miracles?" he said.

"I told you, he's realistic," Fawn said. "Those tortillas could turn into airplanes right in front of us, and he'd say there was some kind of reason for it."

"I think there IS a reason for miracles," said the judge. "There's a reason for every single one that has happened here in Santa Fe."

"You've had miracles here?" Fawn said.

"Well, there's St. Michael's School."

"The boys' high school."

"Right. It burned down in 1926, and the Christian Brothers prayed for the money to rebuild it. On St. Joseph's Feast Day, one of the brothers met a man named Miguel Chavez downtown. When Chavez asked how the building prospects were, the brother told him no money had appeared so far. Chavez said their prayers had been answered—that he had been taken into the school 54 years earlier and credited his education there with making his later success as a merchant possible. He gave them everything they needed right there on the spot."

Will shook his head. "I don't think that's a miracle. That's just a coincidence."

"Interesting," Judge Kohn said. He leaned back and tilted his head at Will. "You don't believe in miracles, and I don't believe in coincidences. Tell you what—would you like to place a little wager?"

"You mean, a bet?" Will said.

He looked at his mother. She gave him a nod.

"I'll bet you that you can't get through the whole summer without seeing at least one miracle."

"You're on," Will said.

He looked at Fawn, but she wasn't looking back at him. Her eyes were suddenly fixed on the front door of the restaurant. Whatever she was seeing, it wasn't good. Her face looked stricken.

Will twisted around and knew why.

Mr. Spitz, the shopkeeper, was standing in the doorway.

Chapter Four

*W*ill reached under the table and grabbed Fawn's knee before she could bolt. She dug her fingers at the tabletop until her knuckles went white.

If God really performed miracles, Will thought, *He'd do one now.*

At the moment, Fawn didn't seem to have too much faith in miracles herself. She slid down in the booth until her chin practically rested on the table.

"Fawn, slither back up, honey," Mom said. "I don't want to lose you under there."

Fawn sat up, but Will could see her looking around for another avenue of escape.

Mr. Spitz was looking around, too. He still stood in the doorway, frowning into the Plaza Restaurant as if he were inspecting it for mice. There was no way he *wasn't* going to see Fawn and Will sitting there. Will held his breath. The disgruntled old man moved his gaze from the counter—to the tables—back to the booths. Across from Will, Fawn gave a tiny whimper.

And then Mr. Spitz suddenly stopped, looked behind him, and abruptly left. But before Will could draw a sigh of relief, he was back, and he was dragging someone behind him by the arm. Will stared. Mr. Spitz was towing Abe into the restaurant.

Abe was still happily waving out the door, apparently to somebody he'd been chatting with while Mr. Spitz had waited impatiently inside.

Even over the chatter of voices and the clatter of forks, Will heard Mr. Spitz bark, "Come on! I've been waiting and waiting while you tend to your foolishness! They don't care about you—you annoy everyone—"

"Lovely man," Mom said, her eyes hard. "I feel sorry for that boy."

"Join the club," Judge Kohn said. "Everyone who's seen them since Spitz moved here says the same thing. He's awfully rough with the boy, especially since he's not altogether bright."

The judge, Mom, and Will watched as Mr. Spitz sat down with his back to them, snatched up his menu, and scowled at it. For a moment, Abe hung his head and appeared to be mumbling something. But when Mr. Spitz paid no attention to him, he looked up and in seconds he seemed to be happy again, mouth half open as he gazed about him, eyes lighting up every time someone glanced his way. Will prayed *he* wouldn't spot them and come bounding over asking if he'd tried out his pillow—the one that was, for all he knew, still lying on the floor of Mr. Spitz's shop, soaking wet.

"Who are they?" Mom said.

"The man's just a cranky old Jew," Fawn said.

"Fawn!" There were no smile-twitches around Mom's mouth. "That is ugly! Why on earth would you say that?"

"That's what the—that's what I heard they say about him."

Will gave Fawn a hard look. She didn't dare look back at him.

"Sorry," she said to her lap. "But he *is* mean—you can tell that."

"Yes, I can," Mom said, "but you don't hear me calling him a name. That's an insult to every nice Jewish person in this town—including Judge Kohn."

Fawn twisted her full mouth at the judge. "Oh," she said. "I didn't mean you."

"No offense taken, little one," the judge said.

"Still," said Mom, "we have to be sensitive. The poor man is both Jewish *and* German."

"You're German, Mom, and you're not cranky," Will said.

"I didn't realize that, Mrs. Hutchinson," Judge Kohn said.

"My parents were both born in Germany," Mom said. "It's been a long time since I even spoke German." She turned to Will. "What I mean is, we have to be careful of the feelings of people like the judge who are worried about their relatives in Europe—with Hitler and his doings. Judge, you were the first one to tell me what they're saying now, about the camps and the gas chambers. Have you heard from your cousins?"

The judge shook his head, and for the first time Will saw what might be sadness in his eyes. Fawn didn't see it. She was busy propping a menu in front of her.

"I hope they've managed to stay out of Hitler's reach," Mom said, as she reached over and took down Fawn's barricade.

"Not many have," said the judge. "You have to consider, six extermination sites have been discovered in Poland alone."

"Extermination?" Will said. "You mean, like killing termites or something?"

"Something like that," the judge said. "Only I think the exterminators of termites are kinder."

"Do you think your cousins were—exterminated?" Will said.

"Will," Mom said, but Judge Kohn shook his head at her.

"It's all right," he said. "The only way we're ever going to prevent something like this from happening again is to tell our young people the truth. Heaven knows the newspapers and magazines aren't doing a good job of it. They've seldom mentioned the killings until recently, and certainly never on the front page."

"We'll put it on the front page of *our* magazine," Fawn said. "Won't we, Will?"

"What?" Will said.

"The magazine you and me are gonna do this summer."

She was nodding so ferociously he thought her head was going to nod right off. He glared at her.

"You two are publishing a magazine?" the judge said.

"I never—"

"Yep," Fawn said. "And if you'll let us interview you right now, you can be our front page story in our first issue."

"I'd be honored," Judge Kohn said.

Will examined his face for signs of *isn't-this-cute*, but he didn't see any. Still, Will gave Fawn one more piercing look and said, "It'll probably never happen. We don't even have a way to print it."

"But that's okay," Fawn said. "Anybody got a pencil? We could all just step outside—"

"No need to do that. Let's just talk right here," the judge said, his eyes twinkling again.

As Mom fished in her purse for a pencil, and the waitress provided a piece of paper from her pad, Fawn looked a little panicked, but Will at last saw what she was trying to do. This could still work, though, if they all kept their heads bent low in conversation—and didn't meet the eyes of either Mr. Spitz or big Abe.

Will leaned way over the table toward Judge Kohn and starting the questioning. Fawn did the same, hanging on every word as if the German Jews were her primary concern in life.

If the judge saw anything strange in that, he didn't let on. He talked for 20 minutes about his cousins from Berlin whom he hadn't heard from in three years and whom he feared had been picked up by the gestapo.

"But it isn't just my own family that concerns me," he said. "It's the fact that our government seems to be doing nothing to help any of the victims of this horror." He shook his head of thinning grayed hair. "I'm afraid there's still a wide streak of anti-Semitism in our country."

Will frowned. "What's that?"

"Anti-Semitism? Hatred of Jews."

"Oh," Fawn said. She seemed to forget herself as she narrowed her eyes at the back of Mr. Spitz's head. "I know one Jew that I—"

"Don't say it, Fawn," Mom said.

"But he's mean!"

Will kicked her under the table.

"That may be true," the judge said, "but it's also true of a lot of Christians—a lot of Hindus—a lot of people who have no religion at all. It simply isn't fair to hate a Jew, or anyone, just because he professes a particular faith. And it's what hate leads to that makes it dangerous to our society."

"I'm just a kid," Will argued. "How could I be dangerous to society?"

"You'd be surprised. They're having one devil of a time up in the Northeast—gangs of kids attacking Jewish schoolchildren. One group of hoodlums stripped a 12-year-old boy to the waist and painted a Star of David on his chest." His bright blue eyes narrowed slightly at Will. "How old are you, Son?"

"I'm 12," Will said.

"Think about it. A bunch of boys from your class wrestles you down on the playground, tears off your clothes and your dignity, and paints a cross on you—just because you don't believe what they believe."

"I'd beat 'em up, all of them," Fawn said fiercely. "If anybody ever tries that, Will, you just let me know and I'll—"

"You'll just calm down," Mom said. She tapped Fawn's plate. "Eat, would you please?"

"I'd much rather see you and Will express that in words rather than with fists." The judge gave her a wry smile. "Though I don't doubt you could probably take on most of Carlos Gilbert Grammar School single-handedly. You do a story about the murders of the Jews in Europe, and I'll buy one of your magazines."

Will watched Fawn squirm in her seat, reach across the table for the chili sauce, and dart a murderous look at the back of Mr. Spitz's neck. She sure had a talent for getting Will into things he'd never have fallen into by himself.

Suddenly Fawn drew in a sharp breath, eyes riveted in the direction of Mr. Spitz's table. Will looked over his shoulder and gasped himself. Abe was pointing right at them and babbling like a kid at the circus.

Will whirled back around. Fawn looked as if she were about to lose her lamb chop.

"Mom!" he said. "Fawn doesn't look so good. I think we better take her home."

Mom looked at Fawn. "That came on rather suddenly, didn't it? What's up, Fawn?"

Fawn looked wildly back at Abe, who Will was sure was probably standing up on his chair by now. Will slid out of the booth and stood up.

"I'm serious, Mom. She looks like she's about to upchuck all over the table."

"We're attempting to eat here," Mom said. She peered more closely at Fawn. "Are you really sick?"

Fawn nodded and threw herself against Mom's chest.

"I'm telling you—we gotta get her outa here or you're gonna be covered in throw-up," Will said.

"*Must* you be so graphic, Son?" Mom said. But she gave Fawn a gentle push toward the end of the bench and looked apologetically at Judge Kohn. "I'm sure you won't be too offended if I take these two home."

Judge Kohn shook his head and stood up so they could all extricate themselves from the booth. Mom finally got her purse on her shoulder, and over the judge's protests she left enough money on the table for their dinners. Fawn kept her face buried against her as they made their way to the front door and, at last, out onto the sidewalk. The fact that Mr. Spitz didn't shout for the police was a good sign, and Will decided it was safe to glance in the window before they drove off. What he saw plunged his heart to the pit of his stomach.

Mr. Spitz was standing up at the judge's now mostly vacant table, waving his arms and pointing toward the door.

Come on, Mom, step on it! Will wanted to shout.

When she did eventually get the Hudson on the way back to Canyon Road, he gave Fawn a nudge and she started breathing again.

"Hey, Mom, what kind of judge is Mr. Kohn, anyway?" he said.

"He's in charge of the family court." She gave Will a sly smile. "Among other things, he tries juveniles that commit crimes, so watch yourselves."

"What's a juvenile?" Fawn said, making a sudden and remarkable recovery.

"A juvenile's a kid," Mom said. She reached over and squeezed Fawn's knee. "Just like the two of you."

✢ ✤ ✢

Chapter Five

Mom's words—and the image of Mr. Spitz telling the whole shoplifting story to Judge Kohn—haunted Will for the next three days. Every time the phone rang, he was sure it was the judge wanting to fill Mom in. Each time the doorbell rang, he was certain it was Officer Perez coming for Fawn.

What are you so worried about? he would ask himself at night when thoughts of their *both* being arrested kept him staring out the window for hours. *Fawn didn't do anything wrong!*

But like Fawn herself, he just didn't want any trouble with Mom. He didn't want her to reconsider her decision to keep Fawn with them, and, besides, Mom was smiling even less than usual these days, as far as he could see. Half the time when he was sitting at the table, telling her all about a baseball game he'd listened to on the radio, he'd realize she hadn't made a comment or even said "Uh huh" for the last five minutes.

"Are you *sure* you didn't tell Mama Hutchie about what happened in the store?" Fawn said to him one afternoon—after jumping down on him from a tree in the backyard and pinning him to the ground.

"Get off me!"

"Not 'til you *swear* you didn't tell."

"She hasn't thrown you out, has she?" Will said.

Fawn considered that just enough to loosen one hand ever so slightly. Will got an arm free and shoved her to one side so he could roll out from under her.

"What's the matter with her then?" Fawn said, pouncing on him again.

"I think she's just worried about my dad," Will said. "We haven't heard anything in a long time."

"Oh," Fawn said. She sat back on her feet. "Ever since my dad went to the war, my mother hardly speaks a word. I guess we're lucky Mama Hutchie talks to us at all, huh?"

But even that stroke of "luck" disappeared that very evening.

The three of them were sitting at the dinner table, eating cornbread and Mom's Spanish rice and chicken casserole, when the phone rang. Fawn dove for it—because having a phone was still a novelty to her—and then handed it off to Mom.

"It's some man," she whispered. "He sounds kind of important."

Will's cornbread immediately stuck halfway down, its spicy chilies burning his throat. "It wasn't Judge Kohn, was it?" he whispered back to her as Mom talked into the phone.

"Nuh-uh. This guy's voice was rough—I don't know, crunchy-sounding."

That didn't make Will feel much better, until Mom suddenly let out a squeal. Will nearly overturned a whole glass of milk. Ingrid Hutchinson *never* squealed.

Mom dropped the phone back onto the hook and untied her apron with one hand while she snatched up her handbag with the other.

"Get in the car, you two," she said.

"Where are we going?" Will said.

"To the train station in Lamy. Your Uncle Al just arrived in town."

Fawn, of course, was full of questions, so on the 20-mile drive through the rolling piñon hills, Mom and Will filled her in.

Uncle Al, they explained, was Will's father Rudy's adopted "brother." Rudy and his twin sister Hildy Helen had been raised by their father and their Great-Aunt Gussie in Chicago. Aunt Gussie had also taken in a boy their age, Al Delgado, who was in danger of going to prison if somebody didn't straighten him out. Aunt Gussie had evidently done that, from all the stories Will had heard, and Uncle Al had become a policeman instead of a gangster, thanks to her.

When the war had started, Uncle Al had enlisted and almost right away he had been selected for the Special Branch. He worked at the Pentagon on what everybody called "intelligence questions."

"Does he wear thick glasses and talk all proper?" Fawn said.

Mom chuckled. "Hardly! He's definitely bright, but an intellectual he is not! Aunt Gussie was never quite able to polish him—although I have to say I'm glad. If anybody can make us laugh, it's Uncle Al."

When they arrived at the station, the squatty wooden depot was bulging with soldiers. One man in an officer's trim uniform rushed through the door, nearly colliding with a baggage man wheeling a suitcase-laden truck, and folded his arms right around Mom.

"Is that Uncle Al?" Fawn said.

"I sure hope so," Will said.

He hadn't seen his uncle since the summer before the war started, when he was nine. But when the man let go of Mom and turned to Will with a lopsided grin and sparkly dark eyes, Will knew it couldn't be anybody *but* Uncle Al Delgado-Hutchinson. He might look polished and important under the shiny brim of his uniform hat, but the tough friendliness was unmistakable, and just as he had when he was a little kid, Will liked him all over again.

"How ya doin', Willie-Boy?" Uncle Al said, sticking out one hand while ruffling Will's hair with the other.

"I'm fine, sir," Will said. He felt his own hand getting lost in his uncle's grip. He wasn't a tall man, but everything about him seemed strong, from his square jaw to his handshake.

Uncle Al grinned widely at Mom. "Your kid just called me 'sir'," he said. "I can see you haven't told him what *I* was like as a kid."

"I heard about it, too," Fawn said. She shrugged. "I bet I coulda taken you, though—if we were kids at the same time."

Uncle Al only stared at her for a few seconds before his grin returned, bigger and more crooked than ever. "I bet you 'coulda.' Who is this little doll, anyway?"

"I'm no 'little doll'!" Fawn said.

But before she could get her fists doubled up, Mom said quickly, "You two kids carry Uncle Al's bags, and let's get him home and fed."

Uncle Al held up a leather satchel. "This *is* my baggage, Mrs. Rudolpho. I'm only here until tomorrow night."

Will saw his mother's face sag.

"Sorry, but that's all the leave I could get. I told you on the phone it was a spur-of-the-moment thing."

"You came all this way for just one day? Why?"

Will glanced anxiously at his mother. There was an edge in her voice that made his stomach do funny things.

"Because I wanted to see you all," Uncle Al said. He flung a husky arm around Mom's shoulders and grinned down at Fawn. "And I heard you had a new little doll livin' with ya. I wanted to see her for myself."

It took most of the way back to Santa Fe to explain about Fawn and to convince Uncle Al that she wasn't a "little doll." Will figured he would always call her that, though. He remembered when he was a little kid, asking why Uncle Al always referred to his mother as "Mrs. Rudolpho." Rudy, she'd told him, had always been "Rudolpho" to Uncle Al, so when she married him, what else could she be?

"I still wish you were staying longer," Mom said as she pulled the Hudson up to the house on Canyon Road.

"When you see how much of your strudel I can eat in 24 hours you won't say that," he told her. Then he turned to Fawn and Will. "If you two will carry this bag to my room, you can have all the candy you can find in it."

"Maybe I *am* glad you're only staying a day," Mom said.

Fawn snatched up the satchel and took off toward the house with it with Will on her heels. Upstairs in the guest room, where the guest bed still looked like an island in a sea of boxes, Fawn tore open the bag, and her mouth fell open.

"There must be five pounds of chocolate in here!" she said. "I guess guys as important as him don't have to ration. Are we really allowed to eat it *all*?"

"Not hardly," Will said. "That's not realistic."

Fawn gazed in rapture at the block of chocolate she was holding. "Then why did he say that?"

"To get us out of the room. He wants to talk to Mom alone."

"How do you know that?"

Will wasn't sure. It was just something he'd picked up over years of being the only kid in a family full of grown-ups. "All the candy you can eat" could only be a bribe, even from Uncle Al. Besides, his mom had seemed nervous all the way home. He could tell by the way the laugh-twitches had disappeared from the corners of her mouth.

"Then why didn't he just tell us to get lost?" Fawn said.

Will shrugged. "I guess he's still always nice to kids because he doesn't have any of his own yet."

Mom yelled for them from below then, and Will started out the door. Fawn paused to grab the rest of the candy.

"I guess they're done talking about grown-up stuff," she said. "Too bad. Mama Hutchie'll notice how much chocolate we really do have and put most of it away."

But the amount of candy Fawn and Will were about to consume was obviously the last thing on Mom's mind. Will could tell that the minute they got to the kitchen and saw Mom's face wrenched tight.

"So you found the stash, huh?" Uncle Al said. "Those are called D-rations. They give 'em to soldiers—loaded with vitamins. A dentist's dream. Why don't you two characters sit down here with us?"

His voice was jovial, like usual, but it sounded to Will like he was having to try hard to keep it that way. Fawn must have noticed it, too, he thought, because she shifted her eyes back and forth between

Uncle Al and Mom even as she sat at the kitchen table and bit off the
first hunk of D-ration.

Will sat uneasily next to her. Uncle Al stayed leaned against the
counter at the end of the table. He had taken off his hat and jacket
and rolled up his sleeves, revealing a pair of muscular arms which he
folded across his chest. He still seemed strong to Will, except that his
face looked as if he had just been called to the front of the class to
recite a poem he'd forgotten to memorize. He looked at Mom with
his brow all furrowed.

"You sure about this?" he said.

Mom nodded. "No secrets from the children," she said.

Wait a minute! Will suddenly wanted to say. *Maybe I* want *whatever this is to stay a secret!* The look on his mother's face was making his stomach more squeamish by the minute. The only thing that
kept him from bolting out of the room was that she wasn't crying.
Surely if Uncle Al were there to tell them his father had been killed,
she would be crying.

Uncle Al gave Mom one more long look. "Okay," he said. "But
anytime you want me to stop, you say so."

She didn't answer him. She just folded her hands on the tabletop
and waited. Uncle Al turned to Will.

"A couple of months ago," he said, "your mother said she'd gotten
a telegram saying your father was a prisoner of war—"

"It said *maybe* he was," Will said. "But I don't believe it. My dad
would never get caught."

Uncle Al closed his eyes.

"Will," Mom said, "let him talk. Then you can ask questions."

"Leave it to Rudolpho to let you *think* he'd never get caught,"
Uncle Al said. He was trying to joke again, and he was having even
less success now. "When we were kids, *I* was the one who never got
caught. He *always* got caught, because he wasn't a fighter. He was an
artist. He always had his head in his visions. I told him he could've
been an illustrator or a designer for the air force and lived in New
York and never even heard a gunshot, but he had to go and sign up

for the 200th Coast Artillery. That was his other problem." Uncle Al
attempted a chuckle. "He would never listen to me, that guy—"

"Why do you keep saying 'was'?" Will said. "You're talking about
him like he's dead! He's not dead—is he?"

"No—no!" Uncle Al put his hand on Will's shoulder. "I was just
trying to keep it from bein' so serious, is all."

"Don't, Al," Mom said. "It *is* serious. Just tell us."

"Tell us what?" Will said.

Uncle Al kept his hand on his shoulder. "I've done some research
for your mother," he said. "It took time because the South Pacific
isn't my area. I study mostly Europe, and people would've gotten suspicious if I'd shown too much interest in something that wasn't my
area."

"Suspicious?" Will said. "Did you do something wrong to find out
stuff about Dad?"

"Are you a spy?" Fawn said.

"I'm not supposed to tell private citizens things I know about the
war," Uncle Al said. "In case the enemy gets the information while
we're passing it out here at home. We have a saying—'Loose Lips
Sink Ships.' But personally, I think sometimes our own people have
a right to know. This was one of those times, so I made a decision
that may not be according to the government's law but it's God's law
to me, if you know what I mean."

Will wasn't sure he did, but he wanted him to go on. He didn't
want to know what he was going to say about Dad, but if he didn't
find out soon, he was sure he'd turn the kitchen table over.

"So here's what I've found out—and your mother says you can be
trusted not to tell any of this to anyone."

Will nodded. So did Fawn.

"Your father's unit was forced to surrender to the Japanese at
Bataan—that's in the Philippines. They fought hard, but they had no
other choice. The Japanese captured them, and they had nothing left
to fight with. Some men escaped. Your father wasn't one of them.
About 76,000 American soldiers and men from the Philippines who

were fighting beside them got herded off about six days after the surrender."

"Herded off?" Will said. "That sounds like cattle."

"That's what it was like, Willie-Boy. They herded them 60 miles." Uncle Al stopped and made a grim face, as if he were finished.

"That's it? That's all you know?" Will said.

"Al, Rudy is our family," Mom said. "We want to know what he suffered. We're part of this."

Uncle Al studied his fingernails. "The Japanese have a warrior code. It's called Bushido. Their pride and devotion to their country is so great that they wouldn't even consider dishonoring their cause by surrendering. They figure any man who surrenders, instead of killing himself first, is the lowest of the low."

He stopped again.

"And?" Will said.

"And—they show no mercy toward men from the other side who surrender *their* cause, either."

" 'Show no mercy'—define that," Mom said. Her voice sounded dead to Will. He was feeling a little dead himself. He had stopped feeling anything in his arms and legs, as if he were separate from them.

"Prisoners who fell out of the march because they were exhausted were bayoneted or shot. Anybody who stopped to try to get a drink of water out of a puddle was beaten."

"Did any of that happen to my dad?" Will heard his voice ask.

"I don't know," Uncle Al said. "But I do know that he made it to the San Fernando railhead and was taken north by boxcar with the rest of the survivors to a prison camp. He wasn't one of the 2,000 Americans who died. And he's accounted for. Ten thousand others still aren't."

" 'Accounted for,' " Fawn said. "What's that mean?"

"That means we know where they are, alive or dead. And Rudy's alive."

"But under what conditions?" Mom said.

Uncle Al didn't answer.

"Al—I want to know."

"I don't know the details—honest, I don't. But I do know that the Japanese soldiers can be cruel. They don't see us as people—we're just the enemy—and the enemy doesn't deserve to be treated like humans, according to them. So they—do whatever they want."

Mom leaned forward, her face set as if it were plaster. "Do they feed them?"

"Just enough to keep them alive."

"Do they have shelter?"

"Like sardines in a can have shelter, yeah."

"If they get sick—"

"If they get sick, they let them die."

Mom sat back stiffly in the chair. Will could no longer feel anything anywhere on his body, except in his stomach. It was surely going to burst wide open any second.

"You wanted me to tell you, Ingrid. But that's all I'm going to say—"

"That's all you have to say." Mom moved her eyes to Uncle Al's face as if they were heavy stones. "He'll never survive that," she said. "You said it yourself—Rudy's not a fighter. He's not strong enough to get through starvation and torture—he won't make it."

She said it so flatly, so without feeling, that it sounded to Will like fact, as if she'd just stated that two times two undeniably equaled four.

"Don't believe her, Willie-Boy."

Will's head jerked toward Uncle Al. He was leaning on the table, his tough hands holding him close to Will's face.

"In the first place, the people I work for are going to start letting more and more of this information out now, to the newspapers and such. We have to get enough determination going to destroy the Japanese empire, and that's going to come from knowing the truth about what's going on over there. And number two—"

He raised a hand from the table long enough to place two

emphatic fingers close to Will's nose. "Your father will never give up the fight to live, because he has too much here at home. I know how much he loves you and your mother. While I was out fooling around, still being a crazy kid, he was *marrying* your mother and taking care of you. He said he wanted to do it because that was what *God* wanted him to do. He was like that when he was 18 years old. You don't think a little hunger's gonna change him now, do you?"

Will wanted to shake his head, but his mother leaned forward, boring her eyes at Uncle Al. "'A little hunger'?" she said. "Face it— he's probably starving to death—and if he isn't, if he does make it home, you know he'll never be the same after all this."

Her voice broke off like a stick snapping, and she got up and left the kitchen. They could hear her footsteps going down the hall to her room. The kitchen was like a tomb for a moment, until Fawn scraped her chair back and stomped to the back door.

"Where are you going?" Will said.

She didn't answer but let the screen door slam behind her.

Uncle Al slumped down on the edge of the table. "I'm sorry, Willie-Boy," he said. "I knew I shouldn't have told your mother, but she kept insisting—she kept writing me letters. I thought she could handle it."

"She *can!*" Will said. "She tells me that all the time—that as long as she's got God she can do anything."

Uncle Al looked up at the ceiling. "I hope she still believes that," he said.

"You said nothing could change my dad. Well, nothing can change her either! It's gonna be all right!"

Uncle Al gave him a long look before he pulled Will's head against the front of his shirt, which was by now damp with sweat, and just held him there. But it was no comfort to Will—because he wasn't sure he believed a thing he'd just shouted at his uncle. Suddenly, it just didn't seem realistic.

✜ ✜ ✜

Chapter Six

*W*ill was awake for a long time that night, even after Fawn came back inside and everyone had settled in. It wasn't a blackout night, so his shade and window were both open to let in the crispy night air. He lay on his stomach on his bed, head in hands, watching the sky twinkle as he thought.

Wonder if Dad has a window where he's sleeping. Wonder if he can ever see the sky, even in the daytime. Wonder if he's scared. Mom thinks he's scared. She thinks he's so scared he's sick, because he's not a fighter. She thinks he'll come home being some stranger or something. Why's God letting all this bad stuff happen?

Will threw himself over to his back and stared up at the models of war planes bobbing at the ends of strings he'd tacked to his ceiling. His thoughts were all bumping into each other. It was confusing—and he hated to be confused. It just wasn't him.

Will flipped back to his stomach and tried to get organized.

Maybe I oughta just ask God outright, he thought. He'd actually started talking to God more since he had met Bud Kates and since just this spring when Mom had told him she was talking to God almost constantly—which might account for the fact that she didn't seem to hear what Will said half the time . . .

But that's not realistic, he thought now. *I'm talking to God every night, and things just keep getting worse. What gives?*

There was no answer. Only a tapping at the door, followed by Fawn padding across his floor in yet another summer bathrobe, blue this time. She went straight to the window as she talked.

"Has he come back?" she said.

"Come on in," Will said. "Don't bother knocking, really—"

"Did he come back?"

She had unlatched the screen and was pushing it so she could lean out the window.

"Who?" Will said.

"That person in that funny-looking car." She was out all the way to her waist by now, and her feet were no longer touching the floor.

"What funny-looking car? Would you watch it—you're gonna fall out."

"You know—that car we saw that night during the blackout. You couldn't tell if it was backing up or going forward, remember?"

Will joined her at the window sill. "He's not gonna come back here—he was probably lost or something."

"Then he musta been lost again tonight, because I saw him."

"When?"

"When I went outside so I wouldn't have to hear any more of those lies your uncle was telling us."

Will blinked at her. He didn't know which direction to go in first.

"I was under the back steps," she went on, "and I heard this car going by and I came out and looked and it was the same one. He was driving real slow. I know he's a spy."

"Good gravy, Fawn," Will said. Impatiently he pulled the screen in and latched it again. "He wasn't a spy. He was just a fella driving around."

"With his headlights off?"

Will looked down at her. She had her arms folded smugly across the front of the blue bathrobe. The lacy collar tossed up in the night breeze and brushed against her cheek, and though she shook it away she kept her eyes on Will, bright and shiny as a pair of buttons.

"Okay, so that's weird," Will said.

"But not for a spy, I bet."

"What would he be spying on us for?"

"That's what we gotta find out, and then we gotta put it in our magazine."

Will's stomach gave him a warning nudge. Magazine. Judge Kohn. Mr. Spitz talking to Judge Kohn.

"We can't be playing around with some dumb magazine right now," Will said. "I just found out my father's in a prisoner of war camp."

Fawn gave the collar a smack as it tickled her face again. "That was a made-up story. Your uncle doesn't know what he's talking about."

"He's in Intelligence! Of course he knows what he's talking about!"

"Nope," Fawn said. "Not his area. He said so himself."

"Why would he make stuff up?"

"I betcha he didn't make it up. I betcha somebody told him that was the truth and he believed them."

Will could feel himself squinting at her. "Like who?"

A satisfied smile spread over the full lower half of Fawn's face. "A Japanese spy. Somebody who *wants* us to think they've got our guys, just so we'll all give up like Mama Hutchie's doing."

For once, Will was having trouble keeping up with Fawn's arguments. He knew his face was so crisscrossed with squint lines it looked like a puzzle.

"My mom isn't giving up!" he said. "What makes you think that?"

"'Cause I saw her looking out her window when I was outside. She was just sitting there doing nothing. Mama Hutchie never does nothing. That's how I know."

"You don't know anything, Fawn!" Will said.

His voice rose over the whisper-level Mom allowed after lights out, and he hunched down his shoulders and waited for Mom to yell from her room. She didn't.

"See?" Fawn said.

"I don't 'see' anything," Will said, setting his jaw.

"You will. We're gonna catch this spy and write about him in our magazine, and we'll let people know it's all just a way to make us give up. Only I'm not gonna."

"It's not realistic," Will said.

"So what?" Fawn said. "Get Mama Hutchie's camera tomorrow. We got work to do."

But the next day was Will's regular day to meet with Bud Kates, and besides, if he'd asked his mother for her camera, she probably wouldn't have answered him anyway.

Since the night before, Mom had fallen into a silence so stony, Will was sure he could have cracked an egg on it, and that obviously made Uncle Al so nervous he wouldn't *stop* talking. At the breakfast table, when Mom snapped that she'd heard *enough* about the war, Uncle Al just clammed up and looked miserable, until Fawn came in and challenged him to arm wrestling. Will heard her pumping him with questions like, "So, do you have many spies where you work?"

They were on round 27 of both the questions and the arm-wrestling when Bud pulled his ancient Chevrolet up out front. Will didn't wait for him to come up to the door. He flew down the front walk yelling, "See ya, Mom," behind him, even though he was sure she couldn't at that moment have cared less. About anything. He was afraid Fawn might be right about her giving up, and that made it more important than ever that he get this God-thing cleared up.

"I got a question for you," Will said almost before he slammed the car door shut. A person had to slam it or it would fly open the next time Bud went around a corner.

"Nice to see you, too, Will," Bud said.

He grinned his sort of sloppy smile, the one Will had once thought was kind of goofy, along with the rest of him. Bud wasn't any Ted Williams baseball champion or anything, that was for sure.

He was pale and pudgy and doughy, and when he had first met him Will had assumed that not only did he *look* like Elmer Fudd but he probably had a personality to match.

But after they'd gotten to know each other some, Will was figuring out that Bud was no ball of dough on the inside. Will had about decided he was smart and strong about a lot of things. Right now he hoped he was smart about God.

Will said, "Can you answer a question?"

"If I can't, are we calling today off?"

Will looked gloomily at the house. "Nah—I don't want to go back in there for a while. Can we go someplace?"

"That was the idea. Three Stooges movie at the Lensic?"

"I've seen it."

"Want to listen to the ballgame over at my place? Tina's got some wieners in the fridge."

Will shrugged. Most of the good players were gone in the service so it almost wasn't worth it, but at least they might be able to talk there.

"I'll take that as a yes," Bud said.

But when they got to Bud and Tina's place, just across from the First Presbyterian Church, Will started talking before Bud could get the car door open.

"Okay," he said. "Why's God letting all this bad stuff happen in the war? I'd started thinking that you and Mom were right, that we could count on God and all that—but I'm thinking it's not realistic."

Bud's pale eyes blinked. "Did I miss something?"

Will opened his mouth, and then shut it. Uncle Al had asked them not to tell anybody.

"I can't talk about it," Will said finally. "We just found out— something bad about my dad. It's *really* bad."

Bud's eyes bulged. "Your father hasn't died, Will?"

"No!" Will said. "It's kinda worse in a way."

He was trying to keep his voice wood-stiff, the way Mom had, as if he were just spitting out dry facts. It seemed to work on Bud, because he just rubbed his chubby fingers on his chin and said "hmm" a couple of times. Will was encouraged. Maybe Bud could clear all of this up after all.

"You know, Will," Bud said finally, "God doesn't bring things like war on us. The inhuman way people treat each other in war doesn't come from God."

"Then why does He let it happen?"

Bud shook his head. "We're not puppets. God's not up in heaven pulling strings. We have choices, all of us, and sometimes we have to deal with the choices other people make."

That wasn't the answer Will wanted to hear. He scowled up at the caving-in ceiling of Bud's car and wished he'd opted for the movie.

"That doesn't help, I take it," Bud said.

"I don't see what good God is, then, if He can't change anything."

"I didn't say He can't. But we have to work with Him."

"Like do what?"

"Pray."

Will sniffed. "I already do that. So does my mom."

"And then we have to expect our prayers to be answered."

"No offense," Will said slowly. "But that's just not realistic. I could ask for my dad to come walking up your driveway right now and expect God to do it, but it'd take a miracle, and miracles aren't realistic."

He thought of his bet with the judge. If Will weren't avoiding Judge Kohn like the German measles, he'd be able to collect on an easy bet at the end of the summer. Maybe he'd do it anyway. After all, Mr. Spitz telling Mom on them was the least of his worries now.

"Miracles *are* realistic," Bud said.

Will looked at him closely. Bud was pulling thoughtfully at his lip.

"You ever seen one?" Will said.

"Yep—and I bet I'll see more. It's just a matter of expecting God to do what only God can do and then listening for instructions."

"Instructions for what?" Will said. "I thought God performed the miracle—I mean, if there is such a thing."

"Wouldn't you like to be involved, though?" Bud said, pale eyes shining. "It's a lot more fun if you're in on it."

"In on what?" Will was starting to get annoyed now. Just sitting through the newsreel at the Lensic would have been worth missing this pointless discussion.

"On whatever miracle you want. What do you want that only God can pull off?"

"My dad home safe and the same as he was before." Will pulled at some of the stuffing that was poking out of the upholstery. "I don't see how God's gonna pull that off, with or without me."

"You don't have to see," Bud said. "Because you aren't God. All you have to do is start praying and expecting."

"But that's not realistic!" Will was wailing by now, which brought Tina's pin-curled head out of the back screen door.

"If that were true," Will went on, "everybody would get everything they want, and that's never gonna happen."

"No, everybody would get what *God* wants," Bud said.

Will yanked a whole tuft of stuffing out. "But what if what I want isn't the same as what God wants? Or somebody else is praying something different and they want it more than I do? Or—"

"Will, my boy," Bud said, "that part of our discussion is going to have to wait. If I don't get you out of this car, you're going to dismantle it."

They went inside, and Bud's petite wife, Tina, served them wieners and gave Will the last few drops of their rationed ketchup. She got on Will's nerves sometimes because she had a habit of squealing a lot, but she was always nice to him. Probably, he'd decided, because she and Bud couldn't have their own kids, so she did stuff for every kid that came in the house so she'd feel like a mom or something. On days when Will and Fawn got under Mom's skin, Mom would say, "Tina Kates doesn't know how lucky she is," and then her lips would twitch. As Will watched Tina bustle around rearranging the wieners on the plate, he wondered if his mother's mouth would ever twitch again.

Bud switched on the radio for the final innings of the Yankees-Dodgers game. Will caught only about half of it. His mind drifted to another score, and so far, no matter what Bud said, the score was Japanese 1, God 0.

Expect God to do what only God can do. Expect a miracle. They still happen.

"Pitcher just walked another player," Bud said, shaking his head.

"It isn't as good with all the good players off fighting someplace," Will said.

But Bud plopped another wiener onto his plate and reached for the mustard. "There's always miracles, you know."

There were no miracles for either the Yankees or the Dodgers that afternoon. The game droned to a boring one-to-nothing at the bottom of the ninth. It almost put Will to sleep.

Until he got home—and saw Judge Kohn sitting, big as life, on the front porch, with Mom.

☩ ☩ ☩

Chapter Seven

*W*ill dug his hand into the seat, right at the place where he'd torn out the stuffing. His fingers snagged on a spring, but he barely noticed. A little pain was nothing compared to the fact that life as he knew it was ending right up there on his porch. Judge Kohn was leaning forward on one of the wooden rocking chairs, talking as much with his hands as he was with his mouth. Across from him, on the swing, Mom was studying her knuckles.

She's embarrassed to even look at him, Will thought. *I shoulda told her myself—instead of letting her hear it from somebody from court, for Pete's sake! As if things weren't bad enough for Mom—*

"Uh, Will."

Will looked up at Bud.

"We're home, pal," Bud said.

"Yeah," Will said miserably.

"That usually means you get out of the car, go up the front walk, say hello to your mother—that kind of thing."

Will watched his mom. Any minute now he knew she was going to call for Fawn—and have the judge just take her away—because she couldn't handle one more thing—

"Something wrong, Will?" Bud said.

Will looked at him. He was leaning on the steering wheel, pale eyes on Will's forehead as if he'd been reading his thoughts the whole time—and understanding them.

I could tell him about Fawn and Mr. Spitz—and I could tell him about Dad in the prison camp—and he might be able to—

Nah.

That wasn't realistic. In the first place, grown-ups obviously stuck together, or Judge Kohn wouldn't be up there on the porch telling on Fawn right now. And in the second place, Bud would just say a bunch of stuff about God working miracles—

If He were going to work one, He'd better start now, because that was what it was going to take to argue his way out of this one.

"Can I help at all?" Bud said.

"No, thanks," Will said. He reached for the door handle, the one that was dangling loosely from its screw. "I'll see ya Sunday."

"I'll see you Saturday night, probably."

"Why?"

"Special prayer service. For the war."

Why do we bother? Will wanted to say. But he muttered a quick, "Sure," and then took as much time as he could climbing out of the Chevy, slamming the door behind him, and ambling across the lawn. Behind him, Bud seemed to linger a little longer than he had to before he finally got the engine moaning and with a pop from the tailpipe clattered off down the street.

Will considered his options as he practically crawled toward the house. He could slip around to the back and at least avoid having his mother yell at him in *front* of the judge. That might make it a *little* less painful. Or he could just make a mad dash for the front door and tell them he had to go to the bathroom bad—and then accidentally lock himself in.

He was about to go with that choice when a tapping sound caught his attention from up above. He looked up at the cottonwood in the front yard, and whatever it was tapped again, but it was coming from the house.

He looked up at Fawn's window, but there was nobody there, nor at his window either. It took one more tap before his eyes went up farther, all the way up to the round window in the attic. The window you couldn't see from inside—

Except Fawn was looking out of it.

She was waving to him frantically, and when she saw that he'd spotted her, she cupped one hand in an exaggerated fashion around her ear and pointed down to the porch with the other one.

She wants me to listen, he thought. He had to admit he couldn't blame her. After all, she had more to lose in this than he did.

Will gave her a small nod, straightened his shoulders, and went straight for the porch. It wasn't until he was halfway up the steps that he realized that one of the wooden posts was concealing a third party in the conversation. Uncle Al.

Rats, Will thought. *Now I've gotta take a fall in front of* him, *too*. The thought of looking like some sneaky little kid to him made Will reconsider.

But it was too late. Judge Kohn raised his chin just then and said, "Here he comes now. Let's just ask him."

This was the worst. All they needed was Officer Perez waiting with his handcuffs to make it completely Will's worst nightmare—and Fawn's.

He tried to swallow a lump the size of a cantaloupe, got rid of about half of it, and took the last three steps in slow motion.

"I can explain everything," he said. "If you'll just give me a chance."

For the first time since Will and Bud had driven up, Mom took her eyes off of her knuckles. They had a distant look in them, as if they'd been a lot farther away than just the backs of her hands.

Will looked quickly at Uncle Al. "I can explain the whole thing, really," he said.

"No need to explain the *whole* thing," Uncle Al said. "Just tell us one thing."

"I'll tell you the truth." Will shifted to the judge. "Honest."

It was then that he saw that the judge's eyes were chuckling.

"You're an intense young fella, aren't you?" Judge Kohn said. "Have you considered becoming an attorney?"

"Put your foot down on that, Ingrid," Uncle Al said. "His grandfather was a lawyer, judge, and we never saw him at the supper table."

Will looked from Uncle Al to his mother. Neither of them had the I'm-about-to-send-you-to-your-room-for-the-rest-of-your-life look. Mom was still gazing through him as if she were someplace else, and Uncle Al was grinning, not the usual face worn when somebody was about to be arrested. Will decided to backpedal.

"What are we talking about?" he said.

"We're talking about whether we can help the Jews in Europe who are being, uh, persecuted by Hitler," Uncle Al said.

Will tried to conceal his relief. It wouldn't be polite to say, "Oh, *that!* Whew!" in front of Judge Kohn.

"*Slaughtered* by Hitler, you mean," the judge said. "I don't think we have to candy-coat things for young Will, do we?"

"No! No candy-coating for me!" Will said. He was afraid he was going to melt into a puddle before he could get upstairs and give Fawn the good news. She probably had her fingernails bitten up to her elbows by now. He edged toward the door. "And speaking of candy—is there any left, Uncle Al, or did Fawn eat it all? I'm starving."

"Just one question, now, Will, since you're a young man who has an opinion on everything." Judge Kohn put a hand on Will's arm, and then curled his fingers around it. Surprised, Will looked into his eyes. He was looking right back, with a knowing gaze that stopped Will in mid-step.

"Sure," Will said.

For some reason, the cantaloupe-lump was building up in his

throat again. The judge's mouth was still smiling, but his eyes weren't anymore.

"Are you anti-Semitic, Will?" he said.

"What's—oh, do you mean, do I hate Jews? No, sir!"

"So—you would never hurt a Jew yourself."

"Well—no. I wouldn't hurt anybody, at least, not on purpose."

"I see," said the judge.

"I could've told you that," Uncle Al said. "He's a Hutchinson—they're all like that."

"Do you know what *passive* means, Will?" the judge said.

"I think it means you just sit there and don't do anything."

"He's a smart boy, Ingrid."

Mom still didn't say anything. She was staring out at the lawn, and yet, Will knew, not really looking at it at all.

"Are you passive, Will?" the judge said.

Uncle Al gave a grunt. "He'd be the first Hutchinson who ever was."

"I don't get what you mean—sir," Will said. Why, he wondered, did he feel as if he were in front of the judge's bench, about to be sentenced?

The judge leaned back and tilted his salt-and-pepper head to the side. "If you knew there were Jews being hurt for no other reason than that they were Jews, right in this town, would you do anything to help them?"

"Well—yeah—I mean, if I knew about it—"

"Say you *saw* somebody do something to a Jew—maybe you saw somebody steal something from a Jewish person—would you speak up? Or would you let it go?"

Will tried to tear his eyes away from the judge's but he couldn't. It was as if their gazes were locked together by some unseen latch. The lump in his throat doubled in size as Judge Kohn watched him, and Will knew: *Mr. Spitz told him. That's what this is about.*

"I'm disappointed in you, Willie-Boy."

The gaze came loose, and Will looked quickly at Uncle Al.

"I didn't think you'd have to consider it for that long," Uncle Al said. "I thought you'd have that answer right there."

"I did—I do!" Will looked back at the judge, and he could feel his eyes begging. "If I saw a person stealing from a Jew or anybody, I'd tell. I would—honest! But that hasn't happened. I know it."

Uncle Al chuckled. "It was just an example, Willie-Boy. Nobody's accusing you of anything."

Will knew his face was going from dead-pale to bright scarlet, and he waved his hand in front of his face. "It's really hot. You mind if I go in and get some lemonade or something?"

Mom nodded vaguely. Uncle Al reached over and ruffled his hand in Will's hair. The judge still watched him with eyes that didn't smile.

"I'm glad to hear that," he said.

"What—that I'm thirsty?" Will said. He sidestepped toward the front door.

"No, that you're not one of those people who appears to be considerate and not anti-Semitic, but who would turn his head if someone else were to mistreat a Jew." He turned to Uncle Al. "You see, that's my point. There's a large body of normally considerate people who are already set up by their hidden negative feelings about Jews to not care about what's happening to them in Europe, nor to care whether our government does anything to help save them."

"I see your point," Uncle Al said.

"I do, too," said Will. "Now—could I go get something to drink?"

"One more thing, Will." Once more, the judge put a restraining hand on Will's arm. It was feeling more like handcuffs each time he did it.

"Yes, sir?" Will said.

"Do you remember that magazine you and Fawn were going to put together—are you still interested?"

"Yes, sir," Will said. It seemed like the safe thing to say.

"So am I. I'll have my office print it up for you, as many copies as you want, if you will make your first feature story a piece about what Americans can do to help the Jews who are suffering in Europe."

"But I don't know anything about any of that—"

"I will help you, of course, and I'm sure Mr. Spitz—you know the owner of that curio shop—I believe we saw him at the Plaza with his grandson the other night—"

Will's lips froze as he formed the next "Yes, sir."

"I think he'd be glad to help you. I know he seems cranky, but perhaps a little interest from you and Fawn would soften that up a bit. What do you say?"

"Uh—sure," Will said. "Sure—yes, sir."

That seemed to be the answer the judge wanted. He let go of Will's arm and gave his shoulder a pat. "Why don't you go see about that lemonade, then?"

Will tried not to lunge for the door. He even said, "Anybody else want some?" But he wanted to get away from this scene just as fast as he could, before the judge dropped another bomb on him.

He took the steps to the second floor two at a time and the ones up to the attic in threes. Once he got there, though, he could only look around lamely. How she'd gotten to the hidden window he still didn't know.

"Fawn!" he whispered hoarsely.

There was a hold-your-breath silence.

"I'm alone," Will said. "Come on, where are you?"

With a squeak, a panel of the wood that lined the attic walls popped free and from behind it, Fawn stuck her head out. The afternoon sun formed a dusty circle of glare before she stepped out and squeaked the panel shut again.

"How'd you find that?" Will whispered.

"I was up here the other day looking at my letters in that box in the floor," she said, "and I got bored and started poking around again, and it just came open."

"How come you didn't tell me?"

"I was waiting to use it to play a trick on you—but forget that now—I had to hide when I saw that judge man coming—"

She stopped talking and flung herself at Will, flattening him to the wall. She wouldn't let him get away until he repeated every word that had been said on the porch twice.

"So Mr. Spitz didn't tell him after all!" she said.

"Don't be a stupe, Fawn," Will said. "Of course he told him. The judge just asked me all those questions because he was trying to decide whether to believe him or not."

"Well, then, I guess the judge doesn't believe him, because he didn't tell Mama Hutchie or haul me off to jail or anything!"

"He *does* believe Mr. Spitz! That's why he's making us go interview him and stuff—that's our punishment, don't you get it?"

Fawn scowled. "Then we just won't do it. Making a magazine was a stupid idea anyway."

"It was *your* idea!"

"Well, now I hate it. We just won't do it."

"I don't think we've got a choice," Will said. He flopped down under the other window. "I think if we don't show up with a magazine to be printed pretty soon, he's gonna think he knows why."

"Why?"

"Because we're afraid to go near Mr. Spitz."

"We *are!*"

"But he's gonna think it's because we're guilty."

"We're *not!*"

Will shook his head. "I don't know why I try to talk to you, Fawn."

"I don't either because you never make any sense."

They both pouted in silence for a few minutes. It was Fawn who couldn't stand it any longer first.

"So I guess we gotta do it," she said.

"Yeah," Will said.

"'Cause I sure don't want Mama Hutchie getting rid of me."

"Yeah."

"She's likely to do just about anything right now—she's in the worst mood I ever saw anybody in."

"Yeah."

"I wish Uncle Al hadn't ever come here."

"Yeah—no!"

"Yes! He's been took over by spies. That's another story we're gonna write about, since we have to do this magazine anyway. We're gonna find out about the spies around here."

"You're nutty."

"You're nuttier."

"Am not."

"Are, too." She crossed her arms, then looked at him sideways. "Speaking of nuts, are there any of those candy bars left?"

✝ ✦ ✝

Chapter Eight

*T*hey consumed their misery in chocolate and almonds. By the time they were licking the last of the remains from their fingers, the judge was gone and it was time to take Uncle Al to the train station.

He looked to Will like a much older version of himself as he climbed into the Hudson for the trip to Lamy. He sat in the backseat with Will—probably, Will decided, because neither Fawn nor Mom was smiling at him much.

"Well, Willie-Boy," he said, "would it cheer you up any to know that a big operation is about to go down in Europe—one that might turn this whole war around for good?"

"Would it mean they'd let Dad go?" Will said.

"Not directly. But it would mean that, with the Germans taken care of, we could concentrate more on the war in the Pacific. And it might be good news for the Little Doll's father."

Fawn whipped her head around, black eyes sharpened to little points.

"I made some calls," Uncle Al said. "Don't worry, Mrs. Rudolpho—I called collect."

He was grinning hopefully at the back of Mom's head. She darted her eyes to the rearview mirror and said, "As if I cared about money right now."

Uncle Al's lopsided smile drooped.

"What about my father?" Fawn said.

By now she was up on her knees, hanging over the front seat, fingers tapping Uncle Al on the knee. Will almost laughed. *What happened to Uncle Al being a liar?* he thought. *She looks like she's ready to lap up whatever he says!*

"He's a part of the Signal Corps," Uncle Al said.

Fawn rolled her eyes. "I *know* that."

"And a pretty important part," Uncle Al added. "I can't tell you how because that's very secret."

"Then what *can* you tell me?" Fawn said. She was nearly crawling over the seat by this time. Will was sure her next move would be to grab Uncle Al by the necktie.

"I can tell you that he's been serving his country very bravely— carrying a pack weighing over a hundred pounds through some pretty rough country. Those radio operators are constantly lugging equipment from place to place, so I know your old man's as strong and brave as any fighting soldier."

"My old man?" Fawn said, brow puckered.

"That's what we called our dads when I was a kid," Uncle Al said.

"Well, go on." Fawn gave him a poke with her index finger.

I'd do it, Uncle Al, Will thought. *Or she'll have you in a stranglehold in a minute.*

"I can tell you that he's working as hard as the infantry. He's under the same harsh conditions they are, but he's making it. All the Navajos, they tell me, are extremely able to adapt."

"What's being a Navajo got to do with it?" Will said. His hackles were beginning to stand up. How come Uncle Al hadn't said all this stuff about *his* dad?

"Some of that I can't answer," Uncle Al said. "The Navajo Indians in the Pacific are often mistaken for Japanese, though. Dark hair, dark skin, not much facial hair, sometimes even Asian-looking eyes. You don't have to worry about that part. Your dad is in France."

"He's in France?" Fawn said.

"He's headed that way, for a very important job. You should be proud of your dad."

Fawn pulled back from Uncle Al's face, chest thrust out, eyes looking superior. "I am," she said. "Of *course* I am."

"He'd be proud of you," Uncle Al said.

"Me? Why?"

"Because you can beat up this guy." Uncle Al thrust a thumb toward Will.

"Nuh-uh!" Will said.

"No—that's not why. He probably doesn't even know about Willie-Boy yet, and I don't know your old ma—excuse me, your father—personally. But I do know that at least one good thing has come out of this war."

"Oh, pray tell, what?" Mom was looking at Uncle Al in the rear-view mirror, her eyes almost in slits. It made Will feel cold all over.

Uncle Al went on slowly, his own eyes on the back of Mom's head. "It's created a place where Indians and whites have to operate on an equal footing. There's no difference between them on the battlefield, and some people say that's going to continue when they get back home."

"*If* they get back home," Mom said. Then she shifted her eyes back to the road.

Uncle Al glanced from Will to Fawn. "*When* your fathers get back home," he said, "they're both going to be proud that you two are putting all racial differences aside and being friends. That's what this war is about, is what I say—getting rid of the hate and living in peace."

"Rudy Hutchinson never hated anybody or anything in his life," Mom said. "So now he's paying for it because other people *do*."

Uncle Al leaned forward. "But Rudy was willing to pay, Ingrid. He was *willing* to go hack his way through jungles and slog through bogs and fight off the mosquitoes—"

"He might have been willing, but he wasn't able. He's not a Navajo Indian! He's a skinny little white boy from Shelbyville, Indiana!"

Mom doubled her hand into a fist and banged it on the steering wheel. Fawn flinched and looked at Will, as if she expected him to tell her what to think. But he didn't know. It looked like Uncle Al didn't either, because he sank back into the seat and shook his head. They were all silent the rest of the way to the train station.

Will hoped that without Uncle Al there as a reminder of what he'd told them, Mom might cheer up again. That didn't happen.

She got busy unpacking the rest of their stuff and planting vegetables in the Victory Garden in the backyard and helping a bunch of volunteer women roll surgical dressings for the Red Cross. Fawn told Will she was glad Mama Hutchie was doing something again.

But Will knew there was a difference now. Mom's eyes weren't laughing. There were no twitches around her lips. And she didn't say sarcastic things when Will and Fawn chewed Juicy Fruit or used too much ketchup on their meatloaf or accidentally rolled the big ball of tin foil they collected for the salvage yard over the geraniums. In fact, she barely seemed to notice.

"She's mad at Uncle Al," Fawn said matter-of-factly to Will Saturday morning when they were deciding which stories to put in their magazine. "You know, because he said your dad's—"

"I know what he said," Will snapped at her. He studied the tip of his pencil. "Do you believe what he said about *your* dad?"

"Of course! He said my dad's practically a hero!"

"So, you believe what he says about *your* father but not what he says about *mine*. I don't think you can do that."

"Why not?" she said. "I'm doing it." She reached over and tried to snatch the pencil from him. "Are you going to write this stuff down or not?"

"I'll do it," Will said. He read over the list they had so far. "Story about spies, story about Jews, story about kale recipes."

"Kale recipes?" Fawn said. She wrinkled her nose. "Kale is

nasty—except the way Mama Hutchie cooks it."

"That's right," Will said. "So we're putting her recipes in there because kale's easy to grow in Victory Gardens, so a lot of people are eating it."

Fawn pondered that for only a few seconds. "Oh. I get it," she said. "What else? Oh—I know!"

"What?"

"We can write about the mystery."

"What mystery?" Will said.

"The one in the floor up in the attic. You know, my Joanna letters."

"That's not realistic. We don't even know what they say."

"That's what makes them a mystery, silly."

Will shook his head. "So when are you going to finish the interview with Judge Kohn?"

Fawn stood up. "Me? I'm not doing it!"

"It's your turn. I had to handle that whole thing on the porch while you hid upstairs."

"I coulda taken him on!"

"Su-ure," Will said. "That's why you were sweating bullets when I found you."

"You didn't 'find' me. I could've stayed hidden forever."

A sulky pause ensued, and then Will said, "All right, I'll make a deal with you. You interview Judge Kohn, and I'll talk to Mr. Spitz."

Fawn scowled at him, but he waited. Slowly her face began to smooth.

"I guess that's not *so* bad," she said. "If the judge didn't yell at you, he won't yell at me. Besides, I don't care what you say, I still think he *knows* I didn't steal that stupid stuff from that cranky old— from Mr. Spitz. I'll go see him tonight."

"You can't. We're going to that special prayer service thing at the church."

"Maybe Judge Kohn'll be there and I can talk to him."

It was Will's turn to roll his eyes. "He's a Jew, Fawn. He's not gonna be there."

"Oh, yeah," Fawn said.

She's gonna drive Judge Kohn nuts, Will thought. And then he felt himself wanting to grin. *But maybe that's good. Maybe he'll wish he never suggested this magazine as punishment in the first place.*

The urge to grin faded. He really did hope so. He really did.

☩ ⋅☩⋅ ☩

Chapter Nine

*T*he church was packed that night and the air felt electric. It was as if everyone was thinking the same thoughts at the same time: *This big operation could change the war—it could bring our boys home.* Even Fawn's face was pensive as she lit her candle and closed her eyes to pray in its flickering glow.

This could bring her *dad home,* Will thought.

He looked up at the high windows that stared like eyes out of First Presbyterian and held back the next thought—about his own dad. He tried to pray, at least for Fawn's father, but he didn't feel anything. That was unusual. Ever since he'd gotten to know Bud— gotten to really know about God—he'd felt that talking to God, to Jesus, was as natural as eating a peanut butter and jelly sandwich. Now, though—

Expect God to do what only God can do, Bud had said. Will tried to pray that, but it didn't seem real, and he was glad when the service was over.

But the waiting for "D-Day", as everyone was calling it, continued to hang in the air like a threatening thunderstorm. The day it was supposed to happen, there seemed to be hardly a person in Santa Fe who wasn't sitting beside a radio when President Roosevelt himself prayed with the nation. Fawn and Will were out collecting scrap metal for the war effort with Will's old red wagon, and they stopped in the doorway of the LaFonda Hotel next to a stand of mariposa lilies to listen to the broadcast, along with all the wealthy tourist ladies in their big flowered hats.

"Almighty God," the president said, "our sons, the pride of our nation, this day have set on a mighty endeavor, a struggle to preserve our republic, our religion, and our civilization, and to set free a suffering humanity."

"My dad's gonna do that," Fawn said.

Five hats turned around and told her "Shhhh!"

"They will need Thy blessings," the president went on. "Their road will be long and hard. For the enemy is strong. He may haul back our forces—"

"No, he won't!" Fawn whispered.

"Success may not come with rushing speed, but we shall return again and again; and we know that by grace and by the righteousness of our cause, our sons will triumph. They will be sore tried, by night and day, without rest—until the victory is won."

All the ladies in the LaFonda lobby said "Amen." Fawn burst into clapping. Will grabbed her by the arm and dragged her and the wagon out of the doorway before the big hats could start shushing again.

"Why can't I clap?" she said, wrenching her arm away. "My dad's gonna be a hero. I have a right to clap!"

Will *really* wanted her to hush up then and was about to tell her so, when his eye caught a flash of color ahead of them at the corner of San Francisco and College Streets. It was *several* flashes of color, actually, and they were worn by three familiar figures.

"Aw—man," Will muttered.

Fawn narrowed her eyes like she was taking aim. She obviously saw what he saw: Luis, Pablo, and Rafael, dressed in too-big suits,

Rafael's bright green, Pablo's a sizzling blue, and Luis's an eye-burning cinnamon brown.

For a minute, Will stopped the wagon and just stared. In the first place, he'd never seen Rafael and company in anything but ragged-looking play clothes, and he'd sure never seen them in suits.

And what suits they were. The coats were nipped in at the waist, and they hung to the boys' knees and had lapels wide enough to act as bulletin boards. The trousers were narrow, like cigarettes, and got more so right at their ankles. It appeared that just wearing them made the three boys swagger even more than usual.

That was the very thing that snapped Will out of his stare, for just then Luis turned his gaze their way and began to strut toward them, his jacket flipping out at the bending of his knees as he approached with Pablo and Rafael at his heels.

"What's the big idea with the suits?" Will murmured to Fawn. "They look like something out of the comics."

"They're gonna look like they just got ripped *outa* the comics in a minute," Fawn said. Her little fists were already poised.

"Let me do the talking," Will said. It was a line he'd heard in a Humphrey Bogart movie, and he'd been waiting to use it.

"I wasn't planning on doing any talking," Fawn said.

"Were you planning on getting in even more trouble by fighting out here on the sidewalk?"

"Okay," Fawn said. "Make it snappy, though. I don't know how long I can hold myself back."

But when Rafael and Luis and Pablo got close enough to stop in front of them, blocking their way, Will saw that none of them looked ready for a battle. In fact, Rafael was poking Pablo, and both of them were looking at Fawn and Will with faces twisted into question marks. Even Luis was cocking a quizzical eyebrow. Will seized the moment.

"Hey, Luis," he said. "What's with this getup? Did you borrow your big brother's suit?"

"Louie the Luck," Luis said.

"You borrowed it from Louie the Luck?" Will said.

"No, An-glow. Mine." Luis jabbed a thumb at one of his wide, cinnamon lapels.

"*Your* name's Louie the Luck? Since when?"

"Since we got us these suits," Rafael said. He edged away from Fawn, who was circling him, inspecting his frog-colored outfit. "I'm Raf the Rough. This here's Pab the Stab."

Will couldn't hold back a snort. "Pab the Stab? How 'bout Pablo the Puny?"

Pablo adjusted his shoulder pads with a shrug. "What's 'puny'? What's that mean?"

"What I wanna know," Rafael said, "is how she got out so fast." He jerked his head at Fawn.

A rough grunt came out of Luis. Will looked at him in time to see his eyes flash at Rafael, who took to adjusting *his* shoulder pads.

"Got outa where?" Fawn said. "What's he talking about?"

Instead of answering, Luis suddenly thrust out one cinnamon-clad leg and kicked Will's wagon. It gave a startled jump and dropped over, dumping its contents. Then he swung the same leg around and took out the stand of lilies. Bruised blossoms scattered on the sidewalk with the scrap metal.

Rafael let out a hard laugh and poked Pablo. Luis grunted at them both and with a jerk of his head sauntered across the street. Pab the Stab and Raf the Rough scurried after him.

"Oh, look at that," said a voice behind Will. It was one of the big-hat women, just emerging from the LaFonda and blinking in the sun's glare at the three Latino boys. "I didn't know they made zoot suits that small."

"Aren't they precious?" said another voice from beneath a hat. "Can't you just picture them doing the jitterbug in those?"

"Oh, yeah," Will muttered to Fawn as he watched the three boys disappear into the knots of post-speech people on the other side of the street.

"Hey kid," said still another voice.

Will and Fawn both jumped. The words came from a scowling man in one of the LaFonda's shiny black vest-and-cumberbund uniforms, and his frown was directed at the spill of old nails and garbage can lids that were currently smashing the lilies in front of his hotel.

"What's the big idea?" he said to Will. "You just ruined 'spensive flowers!"

"I didn't—"

"This is a business establishment. You can't come throw your trash at the plants. You got no respect?"

"But I didn't—"

"This your wagon?" the man said, tapping it with his toe.

"Yeah, but—"

"These your scraps?"

"Yeah, but, see—"

"Oh, I see, all right. I see that you came through here and knocked down private property, and now I'm gonna—"

"Can I help?"

It was yet another voice, and this one Will recognized. Besides, even if he hadn't heard him *or* seen him, he'd have known from the stricken pinch of Fawn's face that it was Judge Kohn.

"No, it's okay, sir," Will said. He dropped to his knees, righted the wagon, and started scooping bits of metal up into his arms. Fawn bent her head so her face was buried in hair and joined him.

Like he isn't going to know who she is! Will thought.

"What seems to be the problem, Manuel?" the judge said above them.

"The ruffians again. I don' know what the town she's comin' to, you know?"

"Oh, I have an idea what it's coming to," Judge Kohn said.

Will squeezed his eyes shut and prayed, but still the judge said, "Why don't you let me handle this, Manuel?"

"Sure, Judge—you go 'head. Just be sure this don't happen again. I gotta million things I gotta do. I ain't got time for this, you know?"

"I certainly do."

"And you be sure these flowers, they get paid for, okay? It takes sometimes three years for these kind to blossom if we gotta drought. This the first time we got rain in a long time."

Will glanced up and saw the judge nod and tip his hat to Manuel.

Will nudged Fawn with his elbow. "Let me do the talking," he whispered.

"Huh," Fawn said, and clamped her mouth shut.

The judge waited until Manuel had gathered up all his injured flowers, inspected the sidewalk for micro-pieces of metal, and hurried back inside to his million things. Then Judge Kohn turned to Will and Fawn. His very bright blue eyes were sharp as he looked at them from under the brim of his hat. Will wondered when he'd exchanged that nice man in the Plaza Restaurant for this person.

"You two just can't seem to stay out of trouble, can you?" the judge said.

"It was an accident," Will said, scrambling to his feet.

"Huh!" Fawn said.

Will nudged her as she stood up to join him. He was beginning to feel like Rafael and Pablo.

The judge studied them for a moment. Then to Will's surprise, he said, "How is your mother?"

"My mother?" Will said. "She's okay, I guess."

"You think she's okay?" The judge's face grew somber. "I *don't* think she's okay. She's very worried about someone she loves, and I know how that feels. I know how much she needs for the people around her to make life as easy as possible for her while she puts all her energy into hoping that loved one comes home. Are you getting this?"

Will was. He could feel his face burning and his cantaloupe-lump forming, and he wasn't sure whether he was angry or embarrassed.

"War's hard on everybody at home," Judge Kohn said. "Maybe hardest on you kids because you have to grow up too fast. Maybe we expect too much of you—but be that as it may, you both need to stay on the straight and narrow, for your mother's sake as much as your own."

Will opened his mouth to tell him how much they were trying—how none of this was their fault—how it seemed like nothing was in their control anymore. But the judge took off his hat and wiped his forehead with the back of his hand, as if that were the end of that topic of conversation and he was ready to introduce a new one.

"How's that magazine coming along?" he said.

"We have a great article on kale," Will said. "And we're kind of—looking for—spies—" He floundered. "And Fawn's gonna interview you—for more information—that's what's holding us up."

The judge nodded. Will could feel Fawn's eyes burning into him.

"Good," said the judge. "How about right now? I have a few minutes."

"Sure!" Will said. He gave Fawn his clearest do-it-or-we're-never-gonna-get-out-of-this look. "I'll tell Mom you won't be home for lunch."

Her fists were doubled up so hard her knuckles were white. Will wasn't sure if they were left over from Luis or newly poised for him.

You'll thank me for this, Fawn, he wanted to say.

But he wasn't so sure about that. He wasn't sure about anything anymore.

Expect God to do what only God can do? he thought as she trailed off after Judge Kohn and he pulled the wagon on toward the salvage yard. *Only God is gonna get a magazine together, get Fawn and me out of this mess, keep Luis and Rafael and Pablo away from us, make Mom her old self again, bring Dad home the same as always—*

But so far, it was the only suggestion he had. He took a deep breath. *I expect it, God,* he prayed.

He looked around. Maybe expecting God to do it *would* work. Maybe Fawn could convince the judge that she was innocent. Maybe Louie the Luck would figure he'd gotten back at Will for good and leave them alone. Maybe that would all happen if he expected it to.

Just to be on the safe side, all the way to the salvage yard down on Galisteo where the fella was collecting the scraps people turned in for the war effort, Will kept an eye out for Luis and Rafael and Pablo, but they weren't part of the crowd of people who were there with their boxes and wagons filled with discarded metal.

"What's goin' on?" one of the shop owner's helpers said. "We got people comin' outa the woodwork today."

"It's D-Day," said a man with a wheelbarrow full of old pipes. "Our boys are over there working for us—we can work for them over here."

"Yeah," somebody else chimed in, "we can win this stinkin' war."

Will decided as he sat in the wagon and rode it back into town, pushing with one foot, that was why there were so many housewives out irrigating their dried-out Victory Gardens. Everybody was inspired by this big operation. Everything was patriotic again, the way it had been at the beginning of the war three years ago.

I guess Luis and those fellas don't care about the war, he thought. *I don't see them out growing their own vegetables.*

He was "driving" the wagon down College Street, when he saw a vaguely familiar figure coming in his direction on the other side of the road.

Why do I think I know that fella? he thought.

But when the boy saw him, Will knew why. He stopped right in his tracks and waved in ecstasy, both arms flailing wildly over his head as if Will could somehow miss seeing him.

Aw, man, Will thought. It was Abe, the boy from the Opportunity School, the sloppy-smile one who wasn't too smart. The one who was Mr. Spitz's grandson—

Will felt a twinge of guilt. If *he* was avoiding going to see Mr. Spitz once, how must Abe feel having to go home to him every single day?

"Poor kid," Will muttered to himself.

But that still didn't mean he wanted to hang around and get slobbered over, and the way Abe was now charging straight at him, it was clear that was exactly what he had in mind.

Feeling a little ashamed, Will looked around for an easy escape route. There was no simple way to disappear, short of jumping into the manhole that was currently gaping wide open in the middle of the street. He wasn't that desperate—yet.

Maybe if I just walk faster he won't be able to catch up with me, Will thought. He got out of the wagon and, grabbing the handle, took off at a trot.

Just then he heard a startled cry from the middle of the street. Will glanced back, just in time to see Abe disappear into the open manhole.

❖ ❖ ❖

Chapter Ten

*W*ill dropped the wagon handle and tore out into the street. Behind him, tires squealed, and a disgruntled voice yelled, "Hey, kid—watch where you're goin'!"

Will ignored the driver as he took the last few steps to the manhole and slid to its edge on his knees.

"Get away from there!" the man called out. "You're gonna fall in!"

"Somebody already did!" said Will.

He was on his belly by now, peering into the hole, but it was so dark he could see nothing but black—until a light suddenly flashed on in his face. Will squinted his eyes.

"Abe?" he said. "Abe—are you all right?"

"I don't know about Abe, but I think *I've* got a broken leg! This kid weighs a ton!"

Will tried peering down into the hole again, and against the glare of the flashlight which the man in the hole was pointing at him he could see Abe's silhouette. That strange language was coming from his mouth again, in excited bursts, as if he were watching fireworks.

"What's he saying?" Will called down.

"How should I know? Get some help, kid. I'm hanging on a ladder down here with a 200-pound fella hanging on top of me. I don't know how much longer I can—"

Will didn't wait to hear the rest. He rocked back on his heels and looked around wildly. The driver who'd nearly hit him had driven on, leaving the street deserted. He didn't even know anybody around here—except—

He hauled himself up from the edge of the manhole and ran like a mad dog toward the shabby little group of adobes that peeked out from behind St. Francis Cathedral. He was already screaming Sister Miriam George's name when he tore past the open-mouthed gardeners out front and flew inside the chicken-house building.

He could hear her crying, "Mercy! Mercy!" before she appeared, black wings fluttering. Her face, framed tightly by its wimple, was bright red.

"Oh, William! William, what is it—what's happened—what's happened?"

Will grabbed at her sleeve. "Abe fell in the manhole—"

"Mercy!"

"A man in there broke his fall, but they need help!"

"Of course! Of course!" she said. But she only managed to turn around in a circle, black sleeves flapping wildly.

"Sister!" Will shouted at her. "Do you have a rope or something?"

"Good heavens, what is going on in *here?*"

Another figure appeared in the doorway, surrounded by little girls with paste-covered hands. Although she was dressed like Sister Miriam George, the figure was as tall and lean as Sister Miriam was short and wide, and she was drawn up so tightly Will was sure she *never* flapped *her* sleeves. She had a stern face, and she peered down at him over the tops of a pair of glasses with chains hanging down from the ear pieces.

"Abe! Abe!" Sister Miriam George cried. "Mary Harold, he's fallen in a hole—fallen right in."

"Well for heaven's sake, haul him out," said Sister Mary Harold.

"We need a rope," Will said. "It's a manhole."

"Good heavens—why didn't you say so? Come on."

Sister Mary Harold did an about-face, practically knocking over half the bevy of little girls with pasty hands. They all darted after the Sister with Will close behind them. But before any of them could even catch up with her, she was back with a rope. They fell over each other trying to get turned around.

"Thanks," Will said, and he tried to take it from her, but she marched back toward the door with it firmly in hand.

"Go back to the puppet-making, girls," she called over her shoulder. "And try to get some of the paste on the puppets this time."

For a second, Will couldn't decide which was a worse disaster: Abe in a manhole or these girls being turned loose with a pot of paste.

"Come on, Son—show me where this manhole is before we lose poor Abe to the depths of the earth," Sister Mary Harold said to him from the front doorway of the chicken house.

"Oh, mercy! Mercy!" he heard Sister Miriam George cry.

"Hold down the fort, Miriam George," Sister Mary Harold said, and she charged on out into the street.

By the time they reached the manhole, the man inside was yelling so loudly he could probably be heard up Canyon Road. Abe was still gurgling away, half talking in that strange language, half laughing. What there was to laugh about Will sure couldn't see.

"Heavens, both of you," Sister Mary Harold said calmly. "Quiet down so I can give you instructions."

"Sister—get a man, would you?" the manhole guy shouted up. "You'll never haul this load of a kid off of me."

Sister Mary Harold leaned over, and her glasses dropped to her chest and dangled from their chain. "Abraham," she said in a dry voice, "grab onto this rope when I lower it, please, and pull yourself up on it so your weight comes off of this nice gentleman. I'm not going to pull you out just yet, so don't try to climb all the way out or you'll kill us all. Do you understand?"

All gurgling ceased. *"Ja,"*—yes—was the reply.

"In English, please," the Sister said.

"I don't care what language it's in, lady! Just get this kid offa me!"

"Quiet," Sister Mary Harold said.

She tossed one end of the rope down into the hole, and Will saw it immediately go taut. The man inside let out a loud gasp of relief. Then she labored with the other end of it to the side of the road, crossed the sidewalk, and wrapped the rope around the trunk of a cottonwood. She looked at Will.

"Come stand here and make sure this doesn't come loose," she said. "The minute it starts to fray or untie, yell like the devil. Do you understand?"

"Absolutely," Will said. There was something about this woman that practically made him want to salute.

He kept an eagle eye on the rope, as promised, though it was hard not to watch Sister Mary Harold as she planted herself about halfway down the rope, took a wide stance with her feet, grabbed on, and called out to Abe, "Pull yourself out, Abraham."

She might as well have been saying, "Get a big grin on your face, Abe,"—she made it sound that simple. Will suddenly had no doubt that Abe would pretty much walk right up out of the hole—and he did, almost.

Just as Will saw his butter-blond head appear, *Abe* apparently saw *him*, because he let go with one arm so he could wave with it to Will.

"*Freund von mir!*" he cried, and fell backwards into the hole.

"What are you doing, idiot!" the man inside shouted. "You were almost out—what's the matter, are you stupid?"

There was a frozen silence in the hole. Sister Mary Harold cracked it open with a voice like an ice pick.

"There will be none of that here, sir," she said. "Abraham is neither an idiot nor stupid. Do you understand?"

"For Pete's sake, lady—"

"Do you understand?"

"Yes!"

"Now, will you kindly shut up so I can pray?"

"Pray? Oh, for Pete's sake—"

"No, sir—for God's sake. Now, if I may?"

"Go ahead—and kid, don't let go again, or I'll—"

Will didn't hear the rest. He was too busy staring at Sister Mary Harold who was poised, hands on the rope, feet digging into the street, with her eyes closed and her mouth forming quiet mutterings.

"I'd give just about anything for an 'Amen' about now!" the man in the hole shouted.

"Amen!" Abe cried happily.

"All right, Abraham, climb with everything you have, Son," said Sister Mary Harold.

Abe did, gurgling from deep in his throat and, when Will could finally see his face, *grinning* with everything he had. He hauled his big body out of the hole, with additional help from Sister Mary Harold, and then proceeded to throw his arms around her. Will shifted from foot to foot. He hoped she'd hurry up and get the other guy out of there before Abe decided to give Will that same hug-treatment.

But getting the manhole worker out was a different task altogether. It didn't take much questioning by Sister Mary Harold to determine that he probably did have a broken ankle, or at least a sprained one.

"I'm going to need some help, Son," she said to Will.

"Didn't I say that? Didn't I say that already?" said the man. "Ow—the pain!"

"I suspect you'll live, sir," Sister Mary Harold said in the direction of the hole. She put her glasses back up on her nose and looked closely at Will. "You look like a sensible sort," she said. "Can I trust you to get a doctor and a couple of strong men? Go to St. Vincent's."

"Okay."

"And take Abraham with you. Don't take him to Sister Miriam George—let's just say that handling crisis is not one of her spiritual gifts."

Will looked at Abe, who was examining a scuffed elbow with his brow bunched up. Wonderful. He was now going to have to drag this big floppy puppy all over Santa Fe. Will half expected him to take his tongue to the scrape on his knee any minute. He looked back at the Sister.

"I don't think I can—"

"And then take him home for some first aid on those scrapes," she said. "He can tell you where he lives."

"Home?" Will said. "*His* home?"

"Unless you want to take him to yours," she said dryly. "Let's hop to it, Son—we have an injured man in that hole."

Without giving him a chance to present even one argument, Sister Mary Harold turned back to the hole and got down on her knees, long black dress and all. Will left before she could start praying, Abe following like an obedient St. Bernard.

"Where we are going?" Abe said as they crossed the street.

"The hospital," Will said.

"No—no hospital! Leg fine—see?"

Abe stopped in the middle of the crossing and happily hiked up a leg for Will to inspect. Will grabbed him by the forearm and dragged him across before an approaching Buick could nick them both.

"It's not for you," Will said between gritted teeth. "It's for the fella in the hole. You fell on him and broke his leg."

Abe stopped again, but this time his big face drooped like a wet dish towel. "I hurt him?" he said.

Will could have bitten his tongue off. "You didn't do it on purpose," he said. "It was an accident."

"I hurt him?" Abe said again.

"You didn't mean to. It was an accident—an accident, okay?"

Good grief, he thought. *No wonder Sister Miriam George says everything twice!*

Abe put a fist up to his own mouth and muffled what he was moaning. Will was sure he wouldn't have been able to understand it anyway. He was talking in that foreign language again. But in the midst of it, a couple of English words tumbled out.

"Bad boy! Very bad boy!"

Then he gargled out some more foreign words and rocked from side to side, his fist still stuck to his mouth. The few passersby were beginning to stare.

Will latched onto his sleeve and tugged. "You're not a bad boy, Abe," he said. "You're a little clumsy—okay, you're a lot clumsy—but you're too much of a big baby to ever hurt anybody."

He immediately wanted to lop off his tongue again, but Abe's face lit up as if Will had just told him he was a dead ringer for Zorro.

"The baby," Abe said, pointing to his chest and gurgling at full throttle. "Baby Abey."

" 'Baby Abey'?" Will said. "That's worse than Pab the Stab. We can think of something better than that. Come on."

He pulled on Abe's sleeve again, and this time the big boy followed, gurgling contentedly all the way to St. Vincent's Sanitarium, bobbing his head at each of Will's suggestions.

"Honest Abe—nah, that's been done. Brave Abe—nope, that's pushing it. Abe the Babe—uh, no."

He still hadn't come up with a name by the time they'd hurried through the big gates at St. Vincent's, found an orderly with big muscles, and explained the situation. Mr. Muscles and another man in white took off at a trot, and Will turned to the next problem at hand.

"So, Abe," he said, "Sister Mary Harold says I'm supposed to take you home to get your cuts looked at, but, see, I don't get along so well with your grandfather, and—"

He stopped. Abe was watching his lips and struggling to form the same words with his own, as if D-Day itself depended on it. His brow puckered up as he looked into Will's eyes.

"Your grandfather," Will said. "I'm supposed to take you to him, but he doesn't like me."

Abe nodded slowly. "Me, too," he said.

"No—he's your grandfather," Will said. "He *has* to like you."

Abe shook his head.

"Yeah, but where else am I supposed to take you to get all those cuts taken care of? You're a mess."

Abe's face immediately fell, and he dropped his head so that his chin rested on his chest.

Good grief, Will thought. *He sure gets his feelings hurt easy.*

Will sighed. "Okay—where do you want me to take you?"

"Home," Abe said. He was already breaking into a grin again.

"But you just said you didn't want to go to your grandfather."

"No," Abe said, shaking his head so hard Will expected to see his eyes wobble. "*Your* home."

"I don't know," Will said. "My mom's in a pretty bad mood. See, my dad's away in the war, and we just got told he's in a prisoner of war camp. I don't believe it, of course, but she does and it's like she's given up, so I don't think she wants any—"

Once again Will stopped. Abe was watching his mouth, trying to keep up, and reflecting Will's own hurt in his big hazel eyes.

"Why am I telling you all this?" Will said.

Abe shrugged happily.

"Good grief," Will said. Then he shrugged, too, and started back toward Canyon Road. "Okay—come on. Maybe you can cheer Mom up—nobody smiles as much as you do. 'Less it's Sister Miriam George."

"George!" Abe crowed.

He gave Will's arm a playful punch, and Will looked at it with interest.

"Maybe you could take Fawn on for me, too," he said.

Abe just grinned.

He doesn't even know what I'm talking about, Will thought. *How do I get myself into stuff like this?*

With another, even heavier sigh, he led Abe toward home. So much for expecting miracles.

✝-✝-✝

Chapter Eleven

*B*y the time they passed the scene of the accident, everyone was gone and the manhole was safely covered up again. Will's wagon was still where he'd left it, and Abe insisted that Will get in so he could pull him home.

Now I feel like an idiot, Will thought. Still, it was better than trying to argue with this big puppy of a person in a debate he couldn't win. Will had come across few people he couldn't outdo in a battle of words. But when Will tried to argue, Abe just stood there watching Will's lips, and then went on doing exactly what he'd been doing anyway. The Sisters had to be patient people. It was a cinch Abe's grandfather wasn't.

Somehow, that thought made Will shiver. Yeah, this was a better idea, bringing Abe home, no matter what kind of mood Mom was in. He just hoped Fawn didn't see Abe pulling Will up the driveway in the wagon.

But Fawn still wasn't home when they got there. There was only Mom, sitting at the kitchen table rolling Red Cross bandages by herself.

"Mom?" Will said as he poked his head in the back screen door.

"You got any extras of those bandages—"

Before he could get the rest of the sentence out, Abe shoved past him from behind and stumbled into the kitchen, bobbing everything he could bob.

"Heim!" he cried. *"Heim!"*

Mom set down the gauze she was rolling and gave Abe a long, slow look, as if she were just waking up from a nap.

"Well, hi there," she said.

Abe bobbed his head and said, *"Guten Tag"* and then charged straight through the kitchen to the pantry and disappeared inside. Mom gave Will a blank look.

"His name's Abe," Will said. "We're supposed to give him first aid because—"

Just then Abe reappeared from the pantry and grinned around the kitchen, big eyes bouncing from the white enamel stove with its shiny black handles to the animals painted on the range hood to the shelves with their red and black and turquoise-colored pottery bowls and pitchers.

Mom turned her blank stare from Will to Abe. He didn't even seem to notice her now, but instead his eyes lit on the door that led to the dining room, and his big lumbering legs followed.

"Will," Mom said as she blinked at the now-empty doorway, "what's going on?"

Abe answered for him from the dining room. When they got there, he was crouched down beside the table, running his hands over the tile floor, and he was muttering again.

"He's speaking German," Mom said.

"What's he saying?"

Mom tilted her head to listen. "He's a little hard to understand—"

"No kidding!"

"But it's something about he remembers this—so cool—so smooth. He keeps saying *Heim.*"

"What's that?" Will said.

"It means 'home'. He must have tile like this at his house."

"I doubt it," Will said. And then the urge to bite his tongue off kicked in.

"Why?" Mom said. "Where does he live?"

"Uh—"

"What's he doing now?"

Abe had stood up and was headed through the wide archway into the living room as if he had a mission. He went straight to the window seat in the front and, to Will's amazement, reached under the cushion and lifted up. The entire top of the seat came up.

"I didn't know that opened!" Will said.

"Neither did I." Mom crossed the living room, saddle Oxfords padding on the bright-colored Navajo rug, and studied the lid Abe had just lifted. He still took no notice of her even being there. He was intent on the compartment he'd just revealed.

"I saw the hinges so I knew it opened," Mom said. "But I searched this whole thing and could never find the latch." She looked at Abe. "You little stinker," she said.

"*Little* stinker?" Will said. "I wouldn't exactly call him that."

"What are you looking for?" Mom said to the back of Abe's head.

He was still inspecting the window seat, running his hands all around the insides of it, poking his head so far inside that his big shoulders nearly disappeared. He didn't answer.

She said something to him in German.

Abe jerked up then, bonking his head on the tilted lid. He didn't even stop to rub it as he faced Mom excitedly and began gurgling away in German. Will could see Mom was having a hard time keeping up, though she did nod here and there. Abe finally stopped and turned his attention to the inside of the seat again.

"What was that all about?" Will said.

Mom nodded her head back toward the dining room and led Will there. She lowered her voice and kept her eyes toward Abe as he continued his search.

"He says it's so good to be home," she half-whispered. "The floor is still cool and smooth and the seat still opens and the sun still comes through like a chute."

"A what?"

"A chute—like a sliding board."

"I don't get it," Will said. "He thinks he's been here before or somethin'. Hey, what's he looking for in the window seat?"

"His pillow," Mom said.

"Oh. He's sure got it bad for pillows." And then he added to himself, *I hope he doesn't ask me where the one is he gave me.* The last time Will had seen it, he was using it to hit Luis in the face.

"Will?" Mom said. "Isn't this the boy we saw in the Plaza that night when we had dinner with Judge Kohn? Isn't he the one the judge said gets browbeaten by his grandfather all the time?"

Will's stomach turned queasy. He looked at his toes for a way to stall. "What's 'browbeaten' mean?" he said.

"Yelled at. Told he's stupid—that kind of thing."

"Yeah—that might be him."

"Excuse me?"

Will looked up to see his mother searching his face, one eyebrow cocked.

"What?" he said.

"You and Fawn were turning yourselves inside out that night so that poor boy wouldn't see you. I'm sure you know if he's the one. Why all the evasion tactics?"

Will didn't have an answer. She'd seen through him like he was a screenless window.

"Well?" she said.

"Yeah, that's him—only that was a while ago, and after all that's happened I kind of wasn't thinking about that."

Good grief! he shouted to himself. *That's* all *you were thinking about!*

"After all that's happened?" Mom said. "Oh—he's headed for my bedroom."

She took off after Abe, who had crossed the entranceway and was plowing into Mom's room, moaning, *"Mutter. Mutter."*

"What's he's saying?" Will said.

"He's calling for his mother."

Mom put her hands up to her face for a moment and closed her eyes. Then she opened them and took Abe by the arm.

"Come on, *Liebschen,"* she said. "Your *Mutter's* not here. Let's see what we can do about this big gash in your elbow, huh? How did that happen?"

Will opened his mouth to tell her, but Abe answered in a gurgling, moaning, grinning combination of German and English and Abe-ese. Mom got him into the kitchen, sitting at the table, and undergoing first aid without a whimper of protest from him.

"Will, help me make us some lemonade," she said as she put on the last piece of adhesive tape.

She patted the bandage and scraped her chair back. Abe leaped up, knocking his own chair backward, and engulfed Mom in a hug that obviously took her breath away. She was gasping when he set her feet back on the floor.

"A simple 'thank you' would do," she said. "No need to throw in a fractured spine for good measure."

Abe gurgled happily and went back to going over the kitchen, knob by knob.

"He's pretty cute," Mom whispered to Will as she picked out a sharp knife for halving lemons.

"Yeah," Will said. He was too stunned to say anything else. Mom's lips weren't twitching at the corners again. She still had that dead look in her eyes. But at least she was talking.

Expect God to do things only God can do. Will grunted to himself.

When Fawn got home, about the time Mom was pouring seconds on lemonade all around, *she* obviously thought Abe was something less than "cute." Fear leaped into her eyes the minute she saw the boy, and Will knew she'd already made the Spitz connection and was planning her escape.

In fact, she was starting to slide toward the door to the back hall, when Mom stopped her with a dry, "Fawn, you know Abe, of course."

"No—"

"Give it up, Fawn," Will said. "She knows."

"She does not!"

"Why are the two of you talking about me as if I'm not in the room?" Mom said.

"Mom knows that we know Abe," Will said quickly. "He kind of had an accident today and she bandaged him up."

Abe proudly showed Fawn his gauze-wrapped elbow, but she barely nodded. She just looked from Will to Mom to Abe.

Mom glanced at the kitchen clock. "Somebody is probably wondering where Abe is by now. We'll take him home in the car."

Will hoped his face didn't look as horrified as Fawn's did. Her eyes clearly said, *Do something—fast!*

"Why don't you let us just walk him?" Will said. "So you can save gas." *We'll just drop him at the door and run,* he assured himself.

Mom looked at Abe who, seemingly unaware of the whole conversation, was contentedly playing with the lemon slice floating in his lemonade. For a moment, her eyes went from dead to sad. "I'd much rather see for myself that all is well when he gets there," she said. "Do you know what I mean?"

"Yes," said Will.

"No," said Fawn.

"Well, one out of two isn't bad,'" Mom said. "Get Abe in the car, would you? I'll go to my room and get my pocketbook."

As Mom turned to leave the kitchen, Fawn gave Will a nudge that nearly cracked a rib.

"Do we have to go, too?" Will said to his mother.

"I think Abe would be more comfortable if you rode along, yes. Wouldn't you, Abe?"

Abe looked up from his glass and quickly pulled his lemonade-soaked finger behind his back. "Sorry," he said, head drooping. "So sorry."

"There's nothing to be sorry for," Mom said. "Put your whole hand in there for all I care."

She gave Abe's head a pat before she left the room. Abe grinned after her as if she'd just turned him into a prince.

"What's he doing here?" Fawn said the minute Mom's footsteps sounded down the hall.

Will pointed to the top of Abe's head and put a shushing finger in front of his lips. Fawn grabbed Will's arm and yanked him into the pantry, swinging the door shut behind them.

"What's going on?" she said.

Will told her. When he was finished, she said, "Find a way so I don't have to go. Talk Mama Hutchie out of it."

"I can't talk to her right now. She's still all—I don't know—stiff and cold," Will said. "I might as well be talking to a gas pump. Besides, I think she wants to make sure old man Spitz doesn't do something to Abe when he gets home."

"I want to make sure he doesn't do something to *me!*"

Will peeked out through the door crack to make sure it was still only Abe who was in the kitchen. He was now poking at the lemon slices in the pitcher.

"What are you gonna do?" Fawn said.

"I don't think I need to do anything," Will said. "I'm thinking about this, Fawn, and—"

"And what?"

"You didn't put that stuff from Spitz's store in your pockets, right?"

"No!"

She made a lunge, but Will put up a hand and she met it with her forehead, fists swinging.

"Cut it out, Fawn!" he whispered hoarsely. "I know you didn't take it—and Mom's gonna believe that. She's still acting funny, but she doesn't like Mr. Spitz as much as we don't like him."

"So?" Fawn said. The word came out like a spit.

"So—if we go there and Mr. Spitz starts accusing us, we just explain to Mom and she'll believe us."

She got so close to his face he could feel her breath on his cheeks. "You think so?" she said.

"Yeah—and when she tells the judge she knows us better than that, he'll believe it, too. Besides, you already did the punishment he gave us."

"Not exactly," Fawn said. Her face was tight.

Will looked at her sharply. "What do you mean, 'not exactly'? You did the interview for the magazine, right?"

"I asked one stinking question about the Jews, and he didn't even answer. He just dragged me into the courtroom and made me sit there all afternoon watching him send people to jail. When he had finally sent about a million people, he said, 'Is there anything you want to tell me, Fawn?' and I said no, so then he said, 'I hope you learned something today.'"

Will's stomach felt as if it were completely turning over.

Fawn shrugged. "I guess *that* was our punishment, but still, if Mama Hutchie even finds out there was trouble in the first place—"

"That's wasn't our punishment!" Will said.

"Don't yell at me, Will, or so help me I'll pin you down so fast—"

"He was trying to show you that he thinks you did it—and what will happen to you if you do it again! He was trying to get you to feel so guilty you'd confess!"

"Then he's just—he's just an idiot!" She stabbed her hands onto her non-existent hips. "He's just a big old stupid idiot!"

"Sorry," said a voice from the doorway.

They both looked up to see Abe filling it, head drooping practically to his belly button, big hazel eyes stung with hurt.

"Sorry," he said again. "Bad boy. Very bad boy. Stupid idiot."

"Hey, we weren't talking about you!" Will said. "Were we, Fawn?"

Whether Fawn would have backed him up, Will didn't have a chance to find out. Abe put his fist to his mouth and began to rock from side to side. He moaned from deep in his throat.

"Look what you did," Will said, turning to Fawn. "He thinks you were talking about him. Abe—"

But when Will turned back to the doorway, Abe was gone. With a disgusted look at Fawn, Will flew out of the pantry and into the kitchen, but he wasn't there either. The back screen door was still swinging shut.

"Abe!" Will shouted as he tore to the back stoop. "Come on back—we don't think you're stupid!"

"What now?" Mom said from behind him.

"He heard us talking about somebody else that was a stupid idiot, and he thought we were talking about him and he took off."

Mom sagged and for a second Will thought she was going to give the whole thing up. But then she hitched her pocketbook strap onto her shoulder and said, "All right—you two stay here. I'll go find him and take him home. And then we're all going to have a little talk."

"I'm not having a 'talk'," Fawn said when Mom drove off with Abe tucked safely into the front seat of the Hudson with her. "I didn't do anything."

"You have to," Will said. "And we're gonna tell her the truth before this gets any worse."

"That's easy for you to say, Will Hutchinson!" Fawn said. Her black eyes were blazing. "She's your for-real mom. She can't get rid of you. But she can get rid of me, and she will if I bring her any more trouble."

"You don't know that. You don't even know my mom."

Fawn's eyes stung with hurt, and for the umpteenth time that day, Will wanted to bite his tongue off, right at the roots.

"I didn't mean it that way," he said. "I know she's Mama Hutchie to you and all that. What I meant was—"

"I know what you meant!"

With one of her trickier lunges, she jumped him and had him pinned under the kitchen table yelling "Uncle" before he could draw his next breath.

"Would ya get off me, Fawn!" he said. "I said 'uncle'!"

"Say 'brother'!"

"Brother? What for?"

"Say you're my brother and you'll protect me no matter what!"

She wrenched his arm back farther and Will gave a grunt.

"You don't need protection—*I* need protection—from *you!*"

"Say 'brother'! I mean it!"

Will tried to turn his head to look at her, but she'd designed the hold so all he could see were the tiles on the kitchen floor. It sure sounded to him like she was about to cry.

"Okay, I'm your brother!"

"Mean it!" she cried with another arm-wrench.

"I mean it, already. I'm your brother—you're my sister—we'll protect each other—okay?"

She finally let go and sat back, leaning against the legs of a kitchen chair. "You didn't just say that because I was holding you down, did you?" she said.

Will sat up and looked at her out of the corner of his eye as he rubbed his reddened arm. There were definitely tears sparkling on her lower lashes.

"No," he said. "You're my sister. Why else would I put up with you?"

"Then you gotta protect me. You can't let Mama Hutchie find out about any of this."

But Will shook his head.

"What do you mean, no?" Fawn said.

"I have a better idea," he said. "I think we oughta find out how that stuff did get into your pockets. I remembered something Mr. Spitz said that day."

"I don't want to hear anything he said," Fawn said, setting her jaw firmly.

"No, listen—he said that wasn't the first time kids had stolen stuff from him. But that was the first time we were ever in his store—ever in our whole lives. So we just gotta find out who *was* stealing, and I think that was the same person who planted the stuff on you."

"Huh?"

"Who else was in the store that day?"

Fawn only frowned for a second before her face lit up. "Luis and those guys!"

"Bingo."

She drew herself up, almost hitting her head on the underside of the kitchen table. Her fists were already in tight little balls. "I'll find them tomorrow and get a confession out of them!" she said.

"Nah," Will said. "That's not realistic."

"I knew you were going to say that."

"You'll only get in more trouble that way. We'll figure something out. And in the meantime, we have to be squeaky clean."

"What does that mean?"

"We can't do anything wrong. We have to be extra helpful to Mom and we have to work on our magazine and do everything we can for the war—so everybody'll know we're good kids."

"Hey," Fawn said. "How come Abe keeps saying, 'Bad boy, very bad boy'? Is he nuts, after all?"

"I don't think so," Will said. "He's okay."

"Yeah, but we have to stay away from him or we're gonna end up right under Mr. Spitz's nose sooner or later."

Will had to agree that she was right, but the thought formed part of that cantaloupe-lump in his throat for some reason he couldn't quite figure out. Fawn nudged him with her toe.

"Are you really my brother, you know, like in here?" she said.

She flattened her hand on her chest. Will felt his cheeks going hot.

"Yeah, sure," he said.

"I don't just want to stay here because I don't want to go back to the pueblo, you know," she said.

Will did *not* want to go on with this conversation. It threatened to become mushy. He climbed out from under the table and looked at the clock.

"Mom oughta be home by now," he said.

The words had no sooner left his lips than there was a knock at the front door. Fawn raced him to answer it—and they both stood there staring as they opened it.

It was Officer Perez.

✟ ◦✟◦ ✟

Chapter Twelve

*F*awn made a move to run the instant she saw the officer standing, hat in hand, on the other side of the screen door. Will
grabbed her wrist and kept his hand curled around it. She stepped
behind him and pried at his fingers.

"Hi, Officer Perez," Will said, forcing his voice to be bright. "My
mom's not here right now—but I could take a message for you."

"I know she's not here," the young policeman said. "That's why
I'm here. There's a problem, and she asked me to come get you two."

Fawn's attempt to pry Will's fingers from around her wrist got
more desperate. He could feel her fingernails digging into his skin,
and he gritted his teeth as he said, "What kind of problem?"

"Why don't you two come with me, and I'll fill you in on the
way?"

At that point, Fawn nearly broke one of Will's fingers bending it
away from her wrist. It was all he could do to hold onto her.

"We're just going to take a little ride," Officer Perez said as he
opened the screen door, "down to police headquarters and—"

That was it. Nothing could keep Fawn from practically snapping
all of Will's fingers in two as she wrenched herself away and cried

out, "I didn't do it! I swear, I'm innocent!"

She tried to bolt, but Officer Perez caught her by the back of her striped polo shirt and neatly picked her up, legs still at a dead run in mid-air.

"Of course you didn't do it. It would be hard to wreck Mrs. Hutchinson's car from inside the house here."

Will froze. "Mom had an accident?" he said.

"Just a minor one. Says she didn't see the car in front of her and just slammed right into him."

Will's stomach was halfway up his esophagus. "Is she hurt?"

"One little cut on the forehead. Come see for yourselves."

Fawn was still shaking her head as Officer Perez set her down, but Will ignored both of them as he hurried past to get to the patrol car. Any other time he would have wanted to know all about the car radio and the siren and the bulletproof shield between the backseat and the front, but the thoughts in his head were so big, they crowded out everything else.

Mom had an accident.

What if she'd been killed or something? What if I lost both Mom and *Dad?*

It hasn't happened, idiot.

But it could.

It so easily could.

When they got to police headquarters on Washington Street, Officer Perez led them straight to a room where Mom sat with her back to them, staring out the window into the rude glare of the afternoon sun.

"Mom?" Will said. "Are you okay?"

She nodded, but when Will went around her chair to face her, he saw that she was anything but okay. A bulky square of gauze had been taped to the middle of her forehead, and there was a circle of soaked-up blood on it. Her face was dead white—except for the smears of wet on her cheeks where she had very obviously been crying. From the looks of her eyes, she was about to again.

"I just wasn't watching what I was doing," Mom said. "I was so lost in thought, I ran right into him. Thank the Lord I had already dropped Abe off. There was no one at his place when I left him—I was thinking about him—and boom—"

"What about our car?"

Mom shook her head.

"Bad?" Will said.

"Very bad."

Will swallowed to get rid of the growing lump in his throat. "But we've got money to get it fixed, right? There's still some left over from what Aunt Gussie left you, right?"

Mom tried to put her forehead in her hands, winced, and sat back in the chair. The tears in her eyes seemed to be making it hard for her mouth to move.

"She could have left us a million dollars and it wouldn't help, Will. The poor old Hudson has seen its last run. It's dead. *Kaput. Fini.*"

"But—"

"And even if she'd left us *two* million dollars, we couldn't buy another one because nobody's making cars because of this—stupid—war!" Her voice teetered. "I hate it! I hate everything about it!"

Will tried to swallow. "Yeah, but—"

"I hate what it's turned people into; I hate that I have to *force* myself to pray because it doesn't seem to do any good; I hate it that every toy, every stick of butter, every grain of sugar has to be rationed—and for what? So your father can rot away in a prisoner of war camp?"

She looked at Will, eyes red-rimmed and demanding, as if she expected Will to give her the answers for all of it. But he couldn't even give her one. He couldn't think of anything except, *Who are you and what have you done with my mother?*

She kicked back the chair and nearly knocked Fawn over getting out of the room. She *was* his mother, and she was scaring him to death.

Expect God to do what only God can do.

I did. I prayed that—but even Mom said it doesn't work! I thought it was working—but now it's just worse. Everything is worse.

He followed Mom out into the hall, but she was already headed for the door.

"What's wrong with her, Will?" Fawn said. She was tugging at her hair like a baby pawing anxiously at its favorite blanket.

"I don't know," Will said. "All I know is, we can't depend on anybody to fix this. We just gotta be extra good. And not just so we'll stay outa trouble. We gotta do it for her."

"I get it," Fawn said. And by the way she solemnly nodded, Will knew she did.

So for the following week and into the next, Will and Fawn concentrated on being model children. It wasn't easy.

Fawn still wanted to wrestle when Will said they should hoe the Victory Garden—because Mom was letting it go to seed.

Fawn still wanted to jump Luis and Rafael and Pablo when they saw them from afar while they were carrying the saved-up kitchen fat to the recycling-for-the-war center—because Mom was just letting the jar overflow.

Fawn still wanted to take a Juicy Fruit break every five minutes when they were out getting people to sign up to donate blood for the Red Cross—since Mom had stopped doing it.

It definitely wasn't just Fawn who had a hard time being perfect. Will had to stop himself from complaining when they had to walk absolutely everywhere or not go at all.

He had to force himself to read the casualty list in the newspaper every day before Mom did, just to make sure Dad's name wasn't on it.

And he had to practically stuff his fist into his own mouth to keep from arguing with Mom when she said for the five-thousandth time in one day that she hated the war.

Hard as it was to watch Mom's lips twitch less and less and see her face pinch in more and more, they both kept trying to brighten things up. Will was glad he had Fawn to do it with.

When the tow truck took the old Hudson away to the scrap heap, the kids hung a sign on it they'd made which said PRAISE THE LORD, I'LL SOON BE AMMUNITION. It was the first mention of the Lord in their house in over a week.

When Will read in *TIME* magazine that Americans had it good during this war compared to England—that Hitler was firing jet-propelled rockets at London and had already killed over 5,000 people right in their own homes—he made it the topic of conversation at the supper table. Mom excused herself before dessert and asked them to clean up the kitchen.

Even when Fawn and Will had a hoot of a time learning all the words to "The Boogie-Woogie Bugle Boy of Company B" and sang it for Mom on the front porch one evening, she said, "Don't they write any songs that *aren't* about this stinking war anymore?" That ended their musical efforts.

Besides, it wasn't long after that that Judge Kohn forced them to do more than just be perfect for Mom.

They were on their way to turn in their ration book at the post office and pick up a new one—watching this way for Abe and that way for Luis and company so they could avoid them all—when they saw the judge coming out of the barber shop, running his hand across his newly trimmed graying hair.

"Just the two people I wanted to see," said the judge. He motioned them over to stand in the shade of the awning over a Navajo rug shop. "I haven't seen any of that magazine you promised me you were going to put together."

"We've been a little busy," Will said.

The judge peered around him at Fawn, who was trying to appear invisible. "Not with the wrong things, I trust," he said.

"Our mom had an accident," Will said. He tried not to sound as annoyed as he felt.

The judge's eyes looked alarmed. "She wasn't seriously hurt, I hope."

"No," Will said.

"She could have been, though," Fawn muttered from behind him.

"But we've been trying to help her, keep her cheered up, just like you said we should," Will said.

"I see. And that's important, certainly." The judge studied them both until Will felt like some legal paper. "I see you're out and about, though," he continued finally. "What do you say you have something on my desk by Friday? Oh, and you haven't forgotten about interviewing Mr. Spitz."

It wasn't a question and didn't seem to require an answer. The judge gave Will's shoulder a pat and, tipping his hat, moved on down the sidewalk.

As soon as he was gone, Fawn reached up and brushed her hand against Will's shoulder.

"What are you doing?" Will said.

"Wiping off where he touched you," Fawn said. "I don't like him. He just needs to go away."

"I don't think that's gonna happen."

"Don't say it—it's not realistic, right?"

"Nope."

"Do you think he'll really tell Mama Hutchie what Mr. Spitz told him if we don't do this?"

"Yep."

So that afternoon they armed themselves with pencil and notepad for Will and camera for Fawn and did the kind of man-on-the-street interviews they'd heard Edward R. Murrow do on the radio.

In as Edward R. a voice as he could mimic, Will said to people in the barber shop, at the counter at Woolworth's, and in front of the post office, "Millions of human beings, most of them Jews, are being ruthlessly gathered up and murdered. Do you think the United States should help them?"

He didn't get the answers he expected.

"Balderdash!" said one man with his face lathered up in the barber chair. "How could the Nazis have murdered millions and us not even know it?"

"Where did you get a story like that?" said the waitress at Woolworth's who was chewing at least four sticks of Juicy Fruit at once.

A man at the post office stuffed his new ration book into his pocket and scowled at the kids. "The best way to help those people is to hurry up and win this war. And after what happened D-Day, I give us another week tops."

It was true that things were looking up since the landing in Normandy on June 6. They'd heard that on the radio. A total of 156,000 American, British, and Canadian troops had gone ashore in 24 hours, leading the way for over two million more men, some of them in the air. There had been problems, Edward R. Murrow had told his audience solemnly, including rough weather and underwater obstacles and 10,000 casualties the first day. Fawn stopped listening at that point.

But still, Murrow assured them, on the second day, the Germans couldn't push the Allies back. General Montgomery and his men were winning. It would be a long fight, just as President Roosevelt had warned them, but all things—the Allies' superior air and artillery power and their many powerful warships at sea—pointed to a sure victory.

After that news, the strict rationing of things like pork and ham and canned fish seemed to ease up a little. Will was glad, since Mom had taken to sending him to Roybal's grocery store because she just didn't feel like leaving the house. It could be confusing, figuring out which items were rationed and whether they had enough tickets left in their book to buy them. A few less of them to worry about was a good thing.

The first time Will brought home three pork chops instead of a can of Spam, Mom raised an eyebrow.

"We can have these now, Mom," Will said, forcing his voice to be cheerful. "That's because we're winning over there."

"Do you think your father is having a pork chop tonight?" she said.

She didn't cook one for herself, and even Will had a hard time getting his down after that conversation.

That night as he lay in bed during a blackout, trying to make out his hanging airplanes in the pitch-darkness, he could still feel the lump. He didn't know if it was the pork chop, or just the fear that was getting bigger every day.

What happened to Mom? he thought. *Why can't she just hope? Why can't she smile just a little or yell at me or make some sarcastic remark I can argue with?*

He was well into his questions before he realized it was God he was talking to. As long as they were talking—

I was expecting, just like Bud said—but You haven't done anything good since—since the day that Abe kid was here. I thought Mom was gonna be all right then, and then she wrecked the car and it was like that wrecked her, too. I don't—

He didn't finish his thought. There was a voice calling outside— what was someone doing yelling during a blackout?

Will went to the window and maneuvered his eye behind the crack between the shade and the window frame. It was far too dark to see anything, but he heard the voice again, and he realized it was coming out of a bullhorn.

"You there! In the Studebaker!" it cried. "Stop! This is the air raid warden—I order you to stop!"

Will pulled the shade out a little farther and squinted down Canyon Road. He could just make out the form of a car, suddenly speeding up in front of the house. Even as he watched, he thought he saw something fly from it onto the front yard. But when he pulled the shade out further still, the bullhorn wailed again.

"Cover that window up there! This is a blackout!"

Will flattened the shade and dove for his bed, heart pounding. Seconds later, his door opened.

"It was your spy again," Will said from under the covers.

"What are you talking about, Will?"

He flinched and peeked over the sheet. It was Mom.

She went to the window and smoothed the shade against the window frame. Then she turned to him.

"Don't make trouble, all right?" she said. "I don't need it. I just don't need it."

"I wasn't, Mom—I—"

"I've had all I can take."

And then she left his room.

Will closed his eyes, and he didn't pray anymore that night. There would be no more praying until he got some questions answered.

✟ ✟ ✟

Chapter Thirteen

*T*he next day was Will's perfect opportunity. It was Thursday, his afternoon to spend with Bud. He was tying on his Keds on the front porch when Fawn joined him.

"Where are *you* going?" he said.

"While you're out with Pastor Bud, I'm gonna look up Luis and them. We have to get started proving I'm innocent."

"I thought we were just gonna do the magazine for Judge Kohn. That's all we need—"

Fawn put her hands on her hips. "I heard Mama Hutchie in your room last night. I heard what she said."

"About what?"

"About how she doesn't need any more trouble. It's not gonna be enough for Judge Kohn to believe us. We have to prove that somebody else did it."

"Don't go by yourself, though," Will said. "Wait 'til I get back."

"No offense, brother," Fawn said, "but I think I'll have more luck on my own."

"What good's tearing them and their little zoot suits to pieces gonna do?"

"I'm not gonna touch 'em. I'm just gonna find them and follow them without them knowing. If other people can spy, so can I."

"What other people?"

"He was out here again last night," Fawn said.

"Who?"

"The man in the funny-looking car. Even the air raid warden saw him."

"You're changing the subject."

"No, I'm not," Fawn said. Her full lips turned up at the corners. "I'm still talking about spying on Luis and Rafael and Pablo. And you're too big to go with me. You can't get in and out of the little places like I can."

Fawn let her grin take up the whole lower half of her face and took off. Within seconds Will couldn't even see her anymore. She did have a way of disappearing. Maybe she *could* spy on Luis and company without them seeing her. Still, it was one of the million things that was regathering into that lump in his throat when Bud pulled the wheezing Chevrolet up to the house.

"Where to today, pal?" Bud said as Will climbed in.

Will shrugged. "No place where I have to try to make anybody laugh or anything."

"Jail."

"No!" Will said.

"That was a joke," Bud said, chuckling. "Just a joke—see, no handcuffs here."

Will felt stupid. "Never mind. I'll go anywhere you want," he said.

Bud put his arm on the back of the seat. "Sounds like you haven't had much luck in the miracle department," he said.

"Forget miracles," Will said. "I'd settle for things just being normal."

"Hmm," Bud said. "We're going to need some of Tina's cherry lemonade for this."

That did sound good to Will. He hadn't had lemonade since the day Abe was over. That was the last day his mother had made it, the last day she'd carried on a real conversation, the last day she'd come close to smiling again.

Too bad I can't bring Abe around again, he thought.

Will considered that as he watched Tina Kates stir cherries into the lemonade and pour it into a jar. But Fawn would have a fit if he took up with Abe, and she was probably right. The farther they could stay away from anything connected with Mr. Spitz, the better. And maybe she *could* get something on Luis and the other thieving little creeps, so Will wouldn't have to interview the old man at all.

Of course, just like everything else that was wrong, that was going to take a miracle.

"All set?" Bud said.

He was standing at the back door with the jar of lemonade and two jelly glasses.

"You sure you don't want some oatmeal cookies with that?" Tina said.

"No, Sugarplum," Bud said. "It's too hot to eat, anyway."

"Then do you have change to get ice cream later?" she said. "I have my ironing money you can use—"

"Sweetheart, that won't be necessary," Bud said.

He nodded Will toward the door. Tina followed as if he'd been nodding to her.

"Now Will, do you have a hat?" she said. "You don't want to get too much sun on that fair skin of yours."

"I won't let him fry—too much," Bud said.

He winked at Will and pushed him on out the door ahead of him.

"I hope you don't mind Tina mothering you," Bud said when they were finally tucked into the old Chevrolet with the lemonade, a blanket to sit on, and several choices of hats. "She just wants a kid so bad. I don't blame her—so do I."

"You can probably have my mother's kids," Will said. "She's not using them."

"Ah," Bud said. "So that's your trouble."

"I guess."

"Oh, I don't guess. I know."

"You couldn't," Will said.

"Let me give it a try. You ask her a question and she doesn't answer because she probably didn't even hear you, even though she's looking right at you. If you mention the war she shoots daggers at you with her eyes. And if you bring up God, she all but leaves the room all together. How am I doing so far?"

"You missed the part about how her mouth doesn't do that twitchy thing anymore. Other than that, you've about got it."

"I thought so. Tina and I can't even get her to come over for a glass of tea. I can only imagine how tough it is on you two kids."

Will was surprised that suddenly there were tears behind his eyes. He looked quickly out the window. Bud was driving them north of Santa Fe, up out of the valley. Behind them a haze of dust hung in the stifling heat. Above, a hawk hung motionless in the sky as if he, too, were feeling, *What's the point?*

But ahead of them the sky was a limitless blue, and the bigness of New Mexico stretched on for miles—the shadowy Sangre de Cristo Mountains to the east of the Rio Grande River, the Jemez mountain range to the west, now shimmering with the sun. There was something about the light in New Mexico that made everything stand out, every needle of every pine tree, every shadow formed by a patch of buffalo grass.

Bud pulled the Chevrolet to a clattering halt just off the road at the foot of a hill and pointed up.

"Ever notice that on your way out to the pueblo?" he said.

Will poked his head out the window. "You mean that big rock thing?" he said. "Yeah—how could I miss it? It looks like a giant camel."

"Must be why they call it Camel Rock," Bud said. "Come on—let's get a closer look."

It wasn't as hot up here as it was in Santa Fe, but Will still broke a sweat as he and Bud carried their blanket, lemonade, and, of course, their hats, up. He was surprised he didn't hear himself perspiring, it was so completely quiet.

All the way to the Jemez Mountains and beyond, the trees were perfectly still. The only things moving were Will and Bud and the occasional critter skittering out from beneath their feet as they walked up the steep slope. The faint pine smell and the surprised lizards were all there seemed to be of life up there—except for Camel Rock. The way its great "head" and "neck" stones teetered precariously on a humped hill made it appear certain that any moment, the gigantic animal was going to stand and take off in long-legged strides between the junipers and the fir trees and piñon pines.

Bud dropped the blanket and gazed up at the Camel. "Nobody can tell me God doesn't have a sense of humor," he said. "Look how comical that is sticking up here in the middle of this great brooding silence."

"What does 'brooding' mean?" Will said.

Bud spread out the blanket and poured them each a glass of cherry lemonade before he answered.

"Brooding," he said finally, "is what you do when you're thinking very deeply about something. And usually that thinking is pretty unhappy."

"Oh," Will said, "like my mom."

"Right. And like you."

Will occupied himself with batting away a bottlefly. Bud just waited patiently.

"I guess so," Will said finally. "I don't know how I'm supposed to be happy. Everything's changing and there's nothing I can do about it." He put a hand up. "And I know you're going to tell me to pray, and I'm doing that—and it isn't making any difference. Far as I can see, things are just getting worse. And I know you're going to tell me to expect God to do things only He can do, but—"

"But what?" Bud said.

"Well, you said I have to work with God, so I've been doing that, but I don't exactly think He's doing His part. I don't know—I just don't think He does miracles anymore."

"You've obviously remembered how I told you to pray and expect."

"Yeah."

"But did I tell you the third part?"

"No."

"You have to listen for instructions."

"Oh." Will tried not to roll his eyes.

"Not realistic, huh?"

"Well—no. I just mean, I don't know how to do that. Is God gonna step out from behind one of those trees and tell me what to do? No, that *isn't* realistic."

"Expect Him anywhere, anytime," Bud said. "He can work through anybody—anything. You just have to be paying attention. Then the miracles can start."

Will set his jelly glass down hard in the dirt. Angry puffs of dust rose from it.

"Why don't *you* do it, then?" Will said.

"I do."

"Then how come no miracles?"

"I've had miracles in my life." Bud grinned his big, sloppy grin. "How else would a beautiful woman like Tina marry a dough boy like me? Or a church call a man who spits when he preaches a sermon?" Bud playfully wiped at the corners of his mouth.

"Why don't you have the kids you want, then?"

Bud stopped wiping. His grin stayed on his lips, but it faded from his eyes.

Will chomped his teeth down on his tongue. "I'm sorry," he said.

"No, it's all right. That's one miracle that hasn't happened yet. But it will, somehow."

"What do you mean, 'somehow'?"

"Maybe it won't happen in the limited way *we* see it, but God sees things so differently. Every day Tina and I look for our answer all around us—in the church, the Bible, the Plaza Restaurant, at the Camel. In you."

"Me? That *would* be a miracle."

"Look, pal," Bud said. "Just pray and expect and look—every-where—in everything. God'll answer. He'll give you instructions that will help you work things out the way they're supposed to be. When He does, that's the miracle."

For once, Will didn't have an argument. In the first place, he couldn't think of one. And in the second—what was the point? Bud believed in miracles. Will didn't.

"You have two choices," Bud said quietly.

Will looked up at him quickly. There was no sloppy grin, no bubbles of spit at the corners of his mouth, no boyish twinkle in his eye. He looked less like Elmer Fudd than he ever had.

"You can fold up and let the enemy win. Or you can pray and expect and keep watch. Your mom is struggling right now, but which one do you think your dad wants you to do?"

Will couldn't answer. The cantaloupe-lump in his throat was way too big.

So for a long time he and Bud sat on the blanket and drank lemonade. Then they hiked all around Camel Rock and dangled their feet in what was left of the Rio Grande. And then they lay on their backs on the blanket again and watched the clouds grow thin like watercolor lines.

"They're getting ready for a spectacular sunset," Bud said. "You can almost feel the expectation—at least I can."

"Do you think my dad ever sees sunsets where he is?" Will said.

"Probably not. Frankly, pal, I don't think your mother's seeing them either."

Will felt the lump coming back, but this time he talked around it. "I don't have two choices," he said. "I only got one."

Bud didn't look at him. He just dug in his pocket for a hand-kerchief and handed it to Will. While Will was wiping his eyes, Bud began to pray.

✛ ✛ ✛

Chapter Fourteen

*I*t was quietly cool when Bud dropped Will off at his house. Bud always said that was the best time in the New Mexico summer, the hour between the heat of the day and the chill of the mountain night. It made Will feel calmer—that and the thought that was now firmly planted in his head: Look for God's instructions everywhere.

"I'll keep praying for Ingrid," Bud said as Will climbed out of the Chevy. "You just keep expecting those directions."

Will stopped, hand on the floppy door handle. "You sure I'm gonna know them when I hear them?"

"If you're paying attention."

Bud smiled his sloppy smile, and Will even managed to grin back. Nothing was any different, but at least he had a plan now. Having a plan—that seemed realistic.

As Bud chugged off in the Chevy, Will shoved his hands in his pockets and walked across the yard. He was looking down, thinking. That was why he noticed something strange lying in the grass. There was just enough sun left to make whatever it was glint. Will leaned over to pick it up—and he froze with his hand on it.

It was a pin, the kind a girl would wear on a blouse. It was made out of cheap silver and had a blob of turquoise glued to it so poorly that as much glue showed as stone.

It looked just like the one Fawn had pulled out of her pocket at Mr. Spitz's store.

The feel of it against his palm made Will shiver. Looking around to make sure no one was peering out a window, he stuck it into his pocket. It felt as if it were burning right through to his skin as he ran up the front steps and into the house.

"Fawn!" he called out.

There was no answer—no sound except the listless clatter of silverware from the direction of the kitchen. Will hurried in. Mom was setting the table, tossing forks and knives at haphazard angles to the plates.

"Hey, Mom, where's Fawn?" Will said.

"I have no idea," Mom said.

"Isn't this her night to set the table?"

"I suppose."

Mom went to the stove and lifted a pot lid. A square of Spam steamed up at her, but she barely flinched. Her eyes looked vague, dim. Fawn disappeared from his mind.

"You want me to go pick some kale?" he said. "There's some coming up."

"I don't feel like cooking it tonight. I think there's a can of peas in the pantry."

"I don't think Dad wants us to stop eating good food just because *he* might not have it."

Mom slammed the pot lid down. "If you can eat kale, Will, you go pick it. If you want a pork chop, you can cook it. But I'm done. Do you understand—I've had it."

No, he didn't understand, but she didn't give him a chance to say so, or to ask a question, or to tell her she was wrong. She *was* wrong, and he wanted to scream that at her. But she yanked the apron from around her waist and flung it down on the table as she stomped from the room. Will didn't wait for her bedroom door to slam before he shoved his way out the screen and let it bang behind him.

"Fawn!" he shouted as he tore around the house and ran down Canyon Road and crossed the bridge.

She didn't answer. What could *she* do, anyway? What could anybody do to bring Mom back? Who was it going to take?

The answer came to him the minute he got to College Street and spotted the manhole cover.

Before the thought could even form all the way in his head, he broke into a run, tearing past late afternoon strollers and startling sleepy mourning doves as he panted his way to the Opportunity School. There *was* somebody there that could help.

But Will's shoulders sagged when he rounded the back of St. Francis Cathedral. The adobe chicken coop was deserted and the yard was empty—except for a tall figure striding across it with glasses dangling from a chain around her neck.

"Good heavens, it's our hero," said Sister Mary Harold.

Will looked behind him to see who she was talking to.

"*You* are a hero, William," she said, putting the glasses on. "That street worker would have let the boy fall and break his neck if you hadn't come along. The attitudes people have about the mentally deficient border on cruel. *You've* obviously had a decent upbringing. Do you go to church?"

Will felt like he was being bombarded, but he said, "Presbyterian."

"Oh," said the Sister. "Well, we won't hold that against you."

Her mouth looked ready to laugh, the way Mom's did—the way Mom's used to. Will felt the lump in his throat.

"Is Abe still here?" he said.

"Heavens, no. He left hours ago. If he isn't home in time to help his grandfather close the store, heaven knows what might happen to him. I'd rather not chance whatever it is, let's just say that."

The lump grew even bigger.

"Is there something I can do to help you, William?" Sister Mary Harold's voice had softened, and her eyes were turned down at the corners.

Look for instructions. Look in everything and everyone.

"I just wanted to find Abe," Will said. "I wanted to take him over to my house."

"How kind of you."

"It's not really me. It's my mom. She likes him."

"How kind of *her*, then." Sister Mary Harold twitched her eyebrows. "She isn't looking for a job, is she?"

"No. She's a teacher. Only it's summer, so she's not working right now. Besides, she's—"

What am I doing? I was about to tell this person all our family business!

Will looked up anxiously. The sun was sinking behind the adobe buildings, leaving them dark and cool with shadows. It was time to just find Fawn and get home and—do what?—open a can of peas?

"The Opportunity School is for all of God's children," Sister Mary Harold said, still watching him through her glasses. "Catholic and non-Catholic alike."

"Yeah, Sister Miriam George told us."

"I don't doubt that. And several times, I'm sure."

"Yeah. She tells you everything several times."

"Well, let me tell it to you again. If you are ever in need of help, even just for an ear to hear you, we're here. You're all God's children, you know."

Will had a sudden urge to hurl himself at Sister Mary Harold's black robe and let her gather him into its folds. But the thought made his cheeks burn, and he backed away.

"Thanks," he said. "I guess I'd better go."

"Have a good evening," she said.

But as he turned and headed back toward the street, he seriously doubted that he would.

"Oh, Son," Sister Mary Harold called to him.

Will stopped and looked over his shoulder.

"There's one thing I forgot to tell you," she said. "If you just want to talk to Abe, it's safe to go see him right now. It's Thursday night.

His grandfather always goes to the temple on Thursday nights. They hold special prayers for the Jews in Europe."

Then she gave him a nod and floated off toward St. Francis with her glasses bouncing from their chain against her chest.

Will stared after her. And then he took off for Mr. Spitz's store.

The shop itself was mostly dark when he arrived, with only some ghostly light spilling down the aisles from a room in the back. Will made his way around to the alley behind the store. At first all he saw was a garbage can—and smelled it as well. As he pinched his fingers onto his nose, he spotted a window. Standing on tiptoes to peer through, he saw Abe sitting in a rocking chair, rocking back and forth and sewing something. In the dim light, it appeared to be one of his pillows.

Will craned his neck to see farther into the back room, but there was no sign of Mr. Spitz. Will raised his hand to knock, then dropped it again. How could Sister Mary Harold be sure that the old man wasn't there? Maybe this wasn't worth the risk.

Will started down the stoop, but then he stopped.

Pray. Expect. Look for instructions. Look in everyone.

What Sister Mary Harold had said, just as he was about to leave, had been the closest thing to instructions he'd gotten.

If Mr. Spitz is here, then I'll just—run, Will thought. *I can outrun that cranky old—*

He stepped back up to the door and rapped on it. There was a slight stirring inside, and then a voice said, *"Grossvater."*

"It's Will, Abe," Will said. What was that thing Abe had called him when he'd seen him at the manhole? "It's *Freund von mir*."

The door flew open and big Abe thrust out his arms and pulled Will into a hug that knocked the breath out of him.

"Hold on!" Will cried. "You're gonna break a rib!"

Abe let go abruptly and stepped back. "I hurt you?" he said. "Bad boy!"

"No—no! You're not bad. I'm fine, see?" He pounded on his own ribs. "Fawn beats me up all the time."

Abe looked momentarily confused, but he broke into a grin when Will grabbed his arm.

"You want to come over to my house?" he said. *"Heim?"*

The big head began to bob, and Abe stepped out the door. But suddenly the bob turned into a shake, and he backed up again.

"What's wrong?" Will said.

"Grossvater," Abe said.

"What does that mean?"

Abe shook his head harder, and shook his index finger, too. "Bad Abe!" he said. "Bad boy—stupid boy. Stupid idiot."

"Oh," Will said. "You're gonna get in trouble if you leave without telling him."

Abe's head bobbed again, and his face dropped sadly. Will had to swallow hard.

"What if we have you back before he gets home?" Will said. "What time does he usually get back?"

Abe blinked. Will stretched his neck and looked around in the room where Abe had been sitting. There was a clock above the corner stove. Will pointed to it.

Abe studied it blankly for a moment, lip hanging, and then with a delighted gasp he ran to it and pointed to the "9".

"He comes home at nine o'clock?" Will said.

"Ja. Neun," Abe said. He clapped his big hands and looked dangerously close to going into some sort of celebration dance. Will tugged at his sleeve and said, "Come on, then. I'll have you back before he ever knows you left."

All fear of *Grossvater* seemed to slip away as Abe closed the door behind him and the two of them hurried through the early evening shadows to the house on Canyon Road. When they got there, the lights had been turned on in the kitchen and, to Will's relief, Mom was slicing the Spam onto a serving plate. However, there was no sign of Fawn.

Will took a deep breath, opened the back door, and gave Abe a gentle shove. It didn't take more than that. The big boy burst through the door gurgling *Heim* and *Mutter* and several other things Will hadn't heard him utter before. That didn't matter. It was the effect it was going to have on Mom that Will was counting on.

She looked up in surprise. She would have had to be a mummy not to. Abe went right to her and put his arms around her shoulders and nuzzled his nose into her neck.

Mom patted his head and raised her eyebrows at Will.

"He followed me home again," Will said. "Can I keep him?"

Abe gurgled gleefully and then once again began his inspection of the kitchen and pantry, as if to make sure nothing had changed since the last time.

"I promise I'll feed him and walk him and make sure he doesn't chew your shoes," Will said.

"Will!" Mom said. "He's not a puppy."

"Yeah, I know. But you said yourself he was cute."

Will was trying to keep the desperation out of his voice. Mom didn't have a smile in her eyes yet, but she hadn't ordered Will to take Abe back where he'd found him either, or worse, ignored him completely.

"No, you can't keep him," Mom said finally.

"Just until nine?"

He could see that she was about to say no. And then Abe clattered back in from the pantry.

"Baby Abey!" he cried, and flopped himself down on the high stool Mom kept near the phone on the wall. "Baby Abey sits here!"

Mom looked at him for so long, Will realized he was holding his breath. Her shoulders relaxed by perhaps an inch, and she shook her head.

"No, Baby Abey," she said. "If you're going to eat, you're going to have to sit at the table with the rest of us. You like Spam?"

Will grabbed a chair and pointed from it to Abe. "From the looks of him, I'll bet he'll eat just about anything."

"Just don't let him eat the tablecloth," Mom said.

But Abe's table manners were better than expected. Definitely better than Fawn's. He waited for Mom to bless the food, and he tucked his napkin into the front of his shirt, and he even waited for Mom to start in on her Spam before he proceeded to wolf his down. Throughout the meal, he bobbed his head appreciatively, as if he were partaking of a banquet at the White House.

Mom didn't say much. She just watched him. That was okay with Will. He was willing to keep the conversation going, even if it meant doing a monologue about anything he could think of while Abe punctuated it with gurgles and German words and various renditions of "Good! Good food!"

Mom did say, "I wouldn't go that far." Then she was quiet again.

She's not yelling, Will thought. *She actually ate some dinner. But, God—I think I need more instructions—um, and fast.*

When the front door opened just then, Will jumped. That was a little *too* quick.

"Must be Fawn," Will said. "I'll go see."

He hurried through the dining room, but Fawn hurtled past him on her way to the back hall. He grabbed her arm and looked at her face.

She looked back out of only one eye. The other was swollen shut with the beginnings of one big shiner.

✞ ✦ ✞

Chapter Fifteen

*W*hat happened to you?" Will whispered.

"Up to the attic!" she whispered back.

She was about to hurtle on to the doorway when Will noticed something else.

"What's that smell?" he said. "Where've you *been*, Fawn?"

"Trying to save our necks!" she hissed. "Meet me in the attic."

She wrenched herself away and disappeared up the steps. Will headed for the kitchen, thoughts racing.

What kinda trouble's she gotten us into this time? Just when I think I might be making some progress with Mom, she makes things even worse someplace else—

Pray. Expect. Listen for instructions.

I'm gonna get instructions from Fawn? he thought. *I'd have better luck listening to Abe, for Pete's sake!*

When he got to the kitchen, Mom had her back to him as she pulled the milk out of the refrigerator. He took full advantage of the situation. Since he didn't hear any instructions, he figured he'd have to fib.

"Fawn's gotta take a bath," he said. "She's filthy from playing—

I'm just gonna take a plate up to her, okay?"

"Sure," Mom said.

She turned just then, and Will couldn't avoid her eyes. There was a slight arching of one eyebrow. She looked as if she were about to say something else, and for an instant Will wished she would. Even if it meant exposing this whole thing, at least it would mean Mom cared—about something.

But the moment passed, and Mom poured milk into Abe's glass. Will grabbed Fawn's empty plate, slapped a slice of now-cold Spam on it with a couple of peas, and hurried out into the hall and up the stairs. He stopped at the bathroom, dumped the food into the toilet, and ran some water into the tub. By the time he finally got up to the secret compartment in the attic, Fawn was like a sack of nerves, tied at the top.

"Get in here!" she hissed.

He squeezed in, and she slid the panel shut. The air in the tiny space was immediately stifling, and the odor oozing from Fawn didn't help.

"Why do you smell so bad?" Will said.

"It was the—"

"And what happened to your eye?"

"I fell—"

"I told you not to follow them alone! Which one of 'em hit you? It was Luis, wasn't it?"

"Nobody hit me—"

"You are such a liar!"

"Will, for once would you just shut up and listen!"

Will stopped, his mouth already halfway into his next question. When the words stopped, the thoughts started. *Listen. Listen to everyone. Listen for God's instructions.*

He took a deep breath, coughed on the stinking air, and said, "What happened?"

She waited a second, watching his mouth. When it didn't move again, she said, "I found them in front of the Palace, you know, where the Pueblos sell things."

"What were they doing?"

"It looked like they were just parading up and down in those stupid suits of theirs. I was going to follow them, except I knew they'd see me so I climbed a tree so I could watch from there."

"And you fell out of the tree?" Will said. "But you never fall—"

"Would you *listen?* I watched them *forever,* and I saw Luis *take* some things from a couple of the women's blankets. Jewelry. When they weren't looking, he'd just pick stuff up and put it in his pockets. You know how big those pockets are—nothing even showed."

"Then what happened?"

"Then he caught up with Pablo and Rafael—'cause they were in different places there at the market—and then they all left."

"Is that when you fell out of the tree?"

Fawn tried to roll her eyes and winced. "No—that's when I *climbed* down and followed them. And you know where they went?"

"Unh-uh."

"The movies! They went into the Lensic Theatre and they musta seen *Andy Hardy's Blonde Trouble* three times because they didn't come out for hours."

"You waited all that time?"

"I went up on the roof of the building across the street to watch for them to come out."

"You fell off a roof?"

"No!"

"Shh!"

Fawn clapped her hand over her mouth. When she talked again, it was in a husky whisper.

"It was starting to get dark and I was about to come home—but I saw Mr. Spitz going up to the window and buying a ticket. He went in the theater, too."

"By himself?"

"Yeah. The third showing of the movie had already started

because a bunch of people had just come out and a bunch more had just gone in. And *then*—"

She stopped to take a huge breath. Will urged her on, his hand beckoning.

"And then," she said, "a couple minutes later, Mr. Spitz came right out again. I guess he doesn't like Mickey Rooney."

"Did Luis and them ever come out?" Will said.

"Not out the front door. Lucky I was on a roof, because just when it was getting *really* dark, I saw something flash down the alley between the Lensic and that shop next door—something bright."

"Zoot suits," Will said.

Fawn nodded. "They musta come out the side exit. I got down off that roof fast as I could, but by the time I did, they were gone. I even asked a couple people if they'd seen 'em, but nobody did."

"How could they miss three zoot suits?" Will said.

"How could *I* miss that garbage can?"

"What garbage can?"

"There's a big one behind old man Spitz's shop."

"I know, but how did you—" Will said.

"I ran there when I lost Luis and them because I thought they mighta gone there—you know, since they were in a stealing mood and maybe they saw Mr. Spitz at the movies so they knew the coast was clear. Anyway, I went back there to see if I could spot 'em and then I heard something and it was a car pulling up so I ran down the alley. Then I heard a voice, and it was Mr. Spitz, and he was yelling."

"What was he saying?"

"I don't know—it was some other language—sounds like he's going to spit all the time."

"German."

"I was looking behind me to see if he was coming, and I ran into the garbage can and tripped and ran right into the corner of the building."

For a second, her face lit into a smile.

"What's funny about that?" Will said.

"He fell over the garbage can, too. I kicked it into his path. That's how I got away."

"Did he see you?"

"I don't think so. It's really dark back there—"

Will suddenly bolted straight up like an exclamation point, banging his head on the top of the compartment. "Oh—man!" he said.

"What's wrong?"

"You ran straight here from there?"

"Yeah."

"That means old man Spitz is home!"

"Yeah."

"And Abe's not!"

"How do you know?" Fawn said.

"Because he's sitting downstairs in our kitchen!"

It was Fawn's turn to sit up straight. Her good eye bulged. "No!"

"Yeah!"

"What's he doing here?"

"I brought him."

"What?"

"Never mind that now," Will said, maneuvering himself around so he could get out of the compartment. "We gotta take him back."

"We? No—*you*. I can't go back there!"

Will stopped, his hand on the panel. "Yeah, you're right. You can't even leave this room or Mom'll see your eye and start asking questions."

"Huh."

Will had the panel open but he stopped to look at her. "What?"

"Mama Hutchie's not gonna care what happened to my eye. She probably won't even notice it."

"It's a little hard to miss!"

"Not when you never look at a person. She hasn't looked at me in days. I bet she didn't even say anything when I wasn't at supper."

Will didn't answer.

"That's what I thought," Fawn said.

"But that's why I brought Abe over here—because last time he came she started to cheer up. And it's working, I think—only now we've gotta—*I've* gotta—get him home or old man Spitz'll probably clobber him."

"Maybe Mama Hutchie could take him. He doesn't know she's our mom—well, your mom."

"She's still your mom!" Will said.

Fawn shook her head. Her hurt eye was growing puffier and darker by the minute but the other one looked just as bad, with sadness pulling it down at the corner and reddening it with tears.

"She *is!*" Will said. "And somehow this is all gonna work out."

"You don't know."

"Yes I do. I'm *expecting* it to."

"How?"

"I don't know that yet." He didn't tell her he just needed to listen. It still sounded so—not realistic. But he could tell her one thing. "I'm your brother, right? We said that."

"Yeah."

"So that means—"

"That means I can trust you," she said.

"Yeah," Will said.

To his surprise, her good eye lit up, and she pulled the lower part of her face into its grin. "So—you want me to hide here 'til you get back?"

"No, just go to bed and pretend you're asleep and maybe your eye will be better tomorrow."

"My grandmother used to say to put meat on a sore eye."

"All we got's Spam," Will said. "I don't think it's the same. But I'll think of something. Oh, and Fawn—"

"Yeah?"

"Take a bath first, would ya? You smell like garbage."

She swatted him with her hand, and he dodged and hurried down to the kitchen.

Mom was dishing up applesauce for Abe when he got there, and the two of them were having a halting conversation in what Fawn would have called that "spit language." Mom looked up at Will, spoon poised.

"You want some?" she said. "It isn't much of a dessert—I need to make some strudel tomorrow."

Will shook his head and began to pry Abe from the chair. "I gotta take Abe home now."

Abe let out a whimper and pointed to the clock over the sink. "*Neun*," he said, shaking his head.

"It's not nine o'clock," Mom said. "That must be his curfew."

"He has to go *now*," Will said.

"Will, it's fine. We were having a nice chat. It was sweet of you to bring him home, and if you have other things to do now, I can entertain him—"

Will couldn't help staring. It was the most she'd said in days. He wanted to sit down and blabber for an hour, telling her all the things she hadn't listened to since the night of the accident and even before. But Abe was happily digging into his applesauce, and there wasn't time now.

"No, it's not that," Will said. "It's—I just remembered he has to be home early tonight."

"Oh—well, it's so dark—why don't you let me walk with you? You and I could talk on the way back—and I think we need to. I'll run up and check on Fawn, and then—"

"No!" Will said. *Where are my instructions, God? Now would be a great time for You to show up*—

"Look, Son, I know what you were doing bringing Abe home, and I want to talk to you about that—"

"Over strudel!" Will burst out. "I'll take Abe home and you make some strudel while I'm gone and—we won't even have to share it with Fawn because she's going to bed—to sleep—right now."

"Strudel?" Abe crowed.

"God love you," Mom said to him. "We'll save you some and you can come back tomorrow, okay?" For a fraction of a second, her mouth twitched. "I'll make a double one," she added.

"Make it a triple," Will said. He pried at Abe in earnest now. "Come on, big fella. We gotta hoof it or your grandfather's gonna—"

Abe froze, his hands gripping the table. The big face he turned up to Will was etched with fear. "*Grossvater?*" he said. "*Grossvater—Heim?*"

"Well, he could be—"

Abe lurched out of the chair, sending the bowl of applesauce one way and the spoon the other. He was at the door, fumbling with the handle, before Will could even take a step.

"Good grief," Mom said. "The poor boy is terrified of that man."

He isn't the only one, Will thought.

Abe was by now out the door and down the back steps. Will took off after him and had a hard time catching him. All the way to Mr. Spitz's shop, Abe's fearful thoughts seemed to double, then triple, then quadruple his speed.

"Stupid boy," he muttered as he trotted down College Street. "Stupid idiot. Bad boy. Very bad boy."

"You're not," Will said, running breathlessly to keep up. "You didn't do anything wrong—this is my fault. I made you come with me."

"No—bad Abe. Very bad."

"No—and I'll tell him, Abe. I won't let him hurt you."

Where those words came from, Will had no idea. But they were out now, and Abe was looking at Will's lips as if to make sure he'd heard right.

Please, God, Will thought as they took the last block to the shop. *Let those be the right instructions I just heard—because I don't know how I'm gonna follow them.*

He was sure he'd never felt fear before like the fear that was turning his stomach inside out and squeezing it.

But what he saw when they reached the curio shop erased that dilemma in one swipe. In its place was the sight of old man Spitz standing in the shop window, shaking his fist—at Officer Perez.

✝ ✟ ✝

Chapter Sixteen

ew words formed rapidly in Will's head.

I've really gotta go, Abe. Here's your home—I'll be seein' ya.

Maybe he would even have said them—if Abe hadn't stopped dead beside him, stuffed his fist into his mouth, and begun to rock from side to side.

Something muffled and mournful came out from around the doubled-up hand. Will didn't have to be able to hear it clearly to know Abe was saying, "Bad boy. Very bad boy. Stupid idiot."

Will's stomach felt as if it were turning completely upside down, but he still said, "You haven't done anything wrong, Abe. Your grandfather probably thinks something happened to you, so he called the police. Nobody's gonna take you to jail or anything."

And nobody's gonna take me, either, he told himself. After all, Officer Perez had believed him last time. Maybe it wouldn't be any different.

"Come on, Abe," he said. "It'll be all right. I'll go with you."

Abe followed him slowly but dutifully up to the front door of the shop, fist still stuck in his mouth, voice still moaning. Will felt like moaning himself, but he kept reassuring Abe—"It's going to be fine. You haven't done anything wrong." His hand shook as he tapped on the window.

Both Officer Perez and Mr. Spitz looked up at once. Nothing registered on the officer's face. But Mr. Spitz's eyes startled open behind his glasses, and his entire head seemed to grow longer and redder as he stared. He was still glaring as Officer Perez opened the door.

Will spewed words as fast as he could get them out. "I brought his grandson back," he said. "I know Mr. Spitz was worried—and it's my fault Abe left—I just wanted him to come to my house—so, anyway, here he is." He reached back to pull Abe into the shop, but the big boy seemed cemented to the front stoop. His eyes were fixed on his grandfather, his mouth still forming the words *stupid idiot*.

But Mr. Spitz had no time for Abe at all. *His* eyes bored right into Will, and then so did his finger. Before even Officer Perez could stop him, the old man had his index finger squarely in the middle of Will's chest and his long nose barely an inch from Will's.

"You! The nerve you have, coming here! You see this nerve, officer?"

Whether Officer Perez saw it or not, Will never found out. Mr. Spitz curled all of his fingers into Will's shirt and yanked Will himself right up into his face. Will's breath fogged the man's glasses.

"Where is the girl—where is that little thief, eh?"

"Hey! Spitz!" Officer Perez said. "Put the kid down, now. Put him down. I'll handle this."

"That's what you said before, and still she comes back!" Mr. Spitz cried. "I catch her prowling around in the back there, tonight—and then I find another pin missing—the kind she likes, eh? If you had handled it before, this wouldn't have happened again!"

"Fawn didn't take your pin before and she didn't take it this time, either!" Will said. "But we know who probably did."

"Who, kid?" Officer Perez said.

"It's three boys that were in my class—they've got it in for me, and Fawn saw them just today, stealing jewelry from the women in front of the Palace. Plus, those same three boys were in here that other day, when all the stuff got knocked over. One of them probably put that pin in Fawn's pocket."

"You gonna give me these kids' names?" Officer Perez said, patting his chest pocket for a pen. "I sure hope so, because, frankly, I'm sick of this whole business."

Will gulped. Officer Perez turned crisply to Mr. Spitz. "We'll check their houses, see if any of your merchandise turns up."

"No!" Mr. Spitz cried. The veins in his temples were bulging. "I want the girl—the Indian girl. This boy is trying to protect her!"

"Look, Spitz," Officer Perez said, his voice sounding as thin as his moustache. "I've got no grounds for taking the kid in, or his friend either—"

"She's not just a friend," Will said. "She's my sister."

"Whoever she is—there's no evidence, Mr. Spitz. It's just your word against his. I'll check out these other kids' homes—"

"Check the *girl's* home!" Mr. Spitz cried. "That's where you'll find my things!"

He jabbed his finger at Will so hard, Will took a step back and tromped right on Abe's foot. Mr. Spitz seemed to see his grandson for the first time. His face darkened.

"Where have *you* been?" Mr. Spitz said.

"Heim!" Abe said.

"Idiot! This is your home!"

Abe cowered. The big hulking mass of a boy hung back against the shop window and cringed as if he were about to be horsewhipped for not knowing where his home was.

"He's just mixed up," Will said. "He was at *my* home—that's what he's talking about."

Mr. Spitz glowered at him. *"Your* home?" he said.

"Yeah. I just took him there because he cheers my mother up—"

"You say that girl, that Indian girl, she's your sister?"

"Yeah." By now Will, too, was confused. He shook his head. "Don't punish Abe. I know he's not that smart and I—"

"Why you took him there? Why? What is the real reason?"

Will didn't even have a chance to get his mouth open. Mr. Spitz snatched him up by the shirt again, this time with both hands, and shook him—again, and yet again—until Will could feel his teeth clacking painfully together.

"Spitz!" he heard Officer Perez cry.

And then he heard something else. They all must have heard it because everyone in the shop was suddenly silent. Even Abe stopped moaning as they stared at the floor. There lay a cheap piece of jewelry, a pin with a glob of turquoise and a glob of glue.

"Where did that come from?" Mr. Spitz cried.

He let go of Will, and before he could stop himself Will felt his pockets. The pin he'd picked up in the front yard was gone.

"Aha!" Mr. Spitz said, his voice rising almost gleefully. "Missing something?"

"No—I—"

"Hey."

Will looked at Officer Perez. His dark eyes were snapping. "Don't lie, kid," he said. "I saw that fall out of your pocket just now."

"It did!" Will said. "I found it, just a little while ago—it was—"

"Don't say anything else," Officer Perez said. "Not until we get you down to the station and get your parents there and sort this whole thing out."

"Parents!" Mr. Spitz said. "There is no father at that house. There is only a mother—who brings in Indians! Savages who take away my business! And the mother—she takes away what belongs to me. It is a houseful of thieves!"

"I have a father—" Will started to say. But he stopped, even before Officer Perez took him by the arm. How did Mr. Spitz know there was no father at his house? Why was he calling Fawn a savage? And why did he say Mom was taking something from him?

There were no answers. No instructions. The only thing he was sure of was that Officer Perez was taking him to jail, and there was no keeping any of it from Mom now.

I'm listening, God—please, he prayed as Officer Perez guided him outside to the patrol car. But there was too much fear in his head for him to hear anything, almost too much for him to *see* anything. Almost.

Except that as Officer Perez started to pull the car away from the curb, another car, driven by Mr. Spitz, roared past them—a car that looked the same in front as it did in back.

"Slow down, Spitz," Officer Perez said to it. "You can't do a thing 'til I get there anyway."

"Is that Mr. Spitz's car?" Will managed to say over the growing lump in his throat.

"Yeah, Studebaker," said the officer. "Silliest looking car on the road—you can't tell if it's coming or going."

Will's heart stopped beating. "Is it the only one in town?"

"Look, kid, you got more important things than that to worry about. You better start thinking about telling the truth when we get to the station." He glanced sideways at Will. "I got you out of this before but I told you to stay away from there, and you couldn't. You're digging your own grave."

"But I'm innocent!" Will said.

Officer Perez grunted. "Innocent people don't carry stolen goods around in their pockets," he said. "You aren't making this easy for me."

Will couldn't speak the rest of the way to Washington Street. The lump in his throat was choking him.

When they got to the station, Officer Perez left him with a bored-looking desk clerk and went off down the hall. Although the clerk didn't seem too concerned about Will attempting an escape, Mr. Spitz stood blocking the doorway, arms folded across a chest that was now soaked in sweat, eyes glittering at Will from behind his glasses. Will's mouth went dry, and he put his fist up to it to stop his teeth from chattering.

No wonder Abe does this, he thought. *No wonder he's so afraid of him.*

There were other thoughts, too—thoughts of Abe moaning at home, thinking this was all his fault and calling himself a stupid idiot. Thoughts of Mom sagging under the weight of one more problem, just when she'd started to come back from wherever it was she'd taken herself. Thoughts of Dad—and how none of this would have happened if he hadn't gone off with the 200th Artillery instead of becoming an air force designer like Uncle Al had told him to. Thoughts of never getting this all straightened out—and him sitting in some jail cell with Pastor Bud coming to pray with him—

Would Pastor Bud still be telling him to pray—and expect—and listen to instructions?

I thought I was doing that, Will thought, wiping his other, sweaty palm on the front of his shirt. *But I guess I wasn't hearing right.*

"Your mother's on her way," Officer Perez said at his elbow. "I just called her."

Will took his hand away from his mouth. "How's she gonna get here?" he said. "We don't have a car now."

"Your mother's having a run of bad luck, isn't she?" Officer Perez said.

But Mr. Spitz interrupted him from his guard post at the door. "Is she bringing that girl—that little Indian thief?"

"I told Mrs. Hutchinson to bring her in," Officer Perez said.

"Why?" Will cried. "Fawn hasn't done anything!"

Mr. Spitz gave a hard grunt and turned to look out the door, as if he were waiting with bated breath to see Fawn in handcuffs. Officer Perez leaned his face close to Will's again.

"I'll do everything I can for you, kid," he said. "But you gotta help yourself. Just tell the truth and get it over with."

Out of the corner of his eye Will saw two figures hurrying up to the door. Mr. Spitz stepped back to let them in: Mom—and Judge Kohn.

Will's stomach seemed to come right up into his throat to meet the fear-lump. It was all over now. They'd obviously already just dumped Fawn off at the jail—either that or Mom had already turned her over to somebody to take her back to the pueblo.

Pray? Listen? Expect?

The only thing he expected now was for Mom to walk over to him and finish the shaking job that Mr. Spitz had started.

She did walk over to him—and then she crouched down, put her arms around his neck, and said, "Will, I know this is my fault. I'm so sorry. I just wish you'd found another way."

Will pulled away to stare at her. Her eyes were glistening with tears, but there wasn't a trace of anger anywhere.

Behind them, Will could hear Mr. Spitz holding forth in spitty-sounding English.

"I told you, Judge, didn't I? I told you those children tried to steal me blind! I told the police—I told you—and what did anybody do about it? Nothing! Nothing—because I am a Jew!"

"And I told *you*," Judge Kohn said, "that I would find out whether Mrs. Hutchinson and her children were anti-Semitic, and I've done that."

"I can tell you what you've found!" Mr. Spitz cried.

"No—I'll tell *you*. Mrs. Hutchinson is as broad-minded and accepting a person as you will ever want to know. I'm honored to be considered her friend."

He nodded his head of thinning salt-and-pepper hair at Mom. From where she was still crouched next to Will, stroking his shoulder, she nodded back.

"As for her children, they've yet to prove their lack of prejudice to me, but so far I've seen nothing to indicate that they would actively hurt a Jew."

The judge shifted his bright blue eyes to Will, who didn't know how to look back. Where was all of this going?

"I have seen it!" Mr. Spitz cried.

"No," said the judge. "There is another explanation for the children's behavior, and I'm going to let their mother give that to you."

Will stared at his mother as she untangled herself from him and stood up.

"Mr. Spitz," she said, "I have never known my son Will to steal anything in his life. Now, Fawn has only lived in my home a short while, but I am responsible for her and I wouldn't have taken that responsibility if I thought she was a thief."

Will's breathing slowed. Of course—that was why Mom wasn't mad. She didn't believe any of this for a second!

"Do you have relatives still in Europe, Mr. Spitz?" she said. "Perhaps family in danger from Hitler?"

Mr. Spitz's eyes blazed out of his long head. "What does that have to do with this?"

"Just answer the question," the judge said. "You'll see."

I hope I see! Will thought.

Mr. Spitz looked around haughtily, as if to determine whether any of them were worth telling. "I have a daughter somewhere in Germany," he finally deigned to say. "And a son-in-law—a stupid idiot—"

"Then you'll understand how I'm feeling," Mom went on. "My husband is right now a prisoner of war, held captive by the Japanese in the Philippines. I have no way of knowing exactly how he's being treated, but from all accounts, it isn't good. If the truth is known, it's probably cruel and savage and torturous, and I can barely sleep at night for thinking about it. In fact, I have hardly been functioning at all these past few weeks, and the worst part of that is that I have neglected my children, obviously to the point where they will do just about anything to get my attention."

Will's heart stopped again, and so did his breathing. Every nerve was straining toward Mom, every cell leaning toward her with the question—*Are you saying what I think you're saying?*

"I'm not excusing their behavior," Mom said. "And it will certainly not go unpunished by me. But I'm asking you not to press charges against them. I'm asking you to allow me to handle this as the mother I should have been to them all along. Would you do that, sir?"

Mr. Spitz didn't even hesitate. "No!" was his reply.

"Come on, man," Judge Kohn said. "I'll vouch for the lady—"

"No! I want this boy put in the custody of the juvenile authorities—and the girl, too. Where is the girl?"

Beside him, Will's mother stiffened.

"We don't know her whereabouts at the moment," Judge Kohn said.

Mr. Spitz very nearly exploded. "You see!" he shouted. "They cannot be trusted! Find the girl—and put them both in the custody of—"

"All right, I will—calm down now—"

Mom's head jerked to the judge. Her eyes were blazing. "What do you mean, you will?" she said.

Will's head jerked, too, as he looked up at her. The voice coming out of this woman was his mother's—his *real* mother's.

"My children are *not* going to jail for taking a couple of cheap trinkets to get my attention! I'll pay for whatever merchandise is missing, Mr. Spit—"

"Spitz! My name is Spitz! Benjamin Spitz!"

"I don't care if it's Franklin Delano Roosevelt! If you were any kind of grandparent to Abe, you would understand exactly how I feel. These are not hardened criminals. This isn't Bonnie and Clyde we're talking about here! These are children who need to be taught, not put behind bars."

"They have sinned against me, and they must be punished!"

"If there's anybody in this room who ought to be punished, it's you—for the abominable way you treat your grandson. In fact, Judge—where do I file a complaint?"

"Ingrid, let's not—"

"I'm perfectly serious. I have never seen a child more terrified of a caretaker in my life. If my children cowered at the mention of my name the way Abe does when he hears *grossvater*, I would gladly hand them over to you this instant and let you put *me* in jail!"

Will could barely suppress a grin. Whatever else happened now, one thing was for sure: Mom was back, and she was fiercer than ever.

But her fire was evidently wasted on Judge Kohn. He ran a hand over his thinning hair and sighed. "As I was saying—all right, Mr. Spitz. I will take both children into the custody of my court."

"And then what?"

"Then we'll see."

"See what? It is clear to me that the children are guilty. One of them has run away, for heaven's sake!"

"I know one thing we need to see about." That came from Officer Perez, who was rubbing his thin moustache as if he were trying to erase it from his upper lip.

"What is it?" Judge Kohn said.

"There's some evidence that there are other kids involved in this. The boy here said so himself. I think we oughta investigate that."

"What other kids?" Mr. Spitz said fiercely. "These are the ones— we got the ones."

"I'll give you the names," Will said. He barely recognized his own voice for the lump in his throat. "I'll tell you anything you want to know. Anything."

Everyone looked down at him as if they'd just realized he was in the room. Judge Kohn nodded.

"All right, Will," he said. "Once you're in custody, I'll hear everything you have to say."

"Judge!" Mom said.

She looked wild-eyed, but the judge just nodded to the policeman. Officer Perez started toward Will with the handcuffs in his hands.

‡⋅‡⋅‡

Chapter Seventeen

*Y*ou will *not* put those handcuffs on my child!" Ingrid
Hutchinson said. "He is *not* a criminal!"

"He stole from me! He is a thief!" said Mr. Spitz. "Where I
come from, they call that a criminal!"

"Where you come from, they put people in gas chambers for—"

"All right—enough."

The room got quiet. The judge had his hand up, his shoulders
squared. Will had an instant image of what he must look like commanding from his bench in the courtroom, and it made him shudder.

"I am taking the boy into custody," Judge Kohn said. "But, Perez,
there will be no need for cuffs. I think he'll come quietly."

Come quietly? Will thought as he rubbed his wrist. *I'm so quiet
they're gonna have to carry me out of here. I think I'm paralyzed!*

But his legs did move as Officer Perez took him gently by the
arm and ushered him through a door behind the clerk's desk.

"Judge—" he heard Mom say behind him.

"Trust me, Ingrid," Judge Kohn said.

"I don't trust you!" Mr. Spitz cried. "I don't trust you one bit. I
want to *see* the boy behind bars."

"You've seen all you're going to see," Judge Kohn said. "Go home to your grandson."

Whatever else was said, Will didn't hear. A door slammed behind him, and Will's knees buckled. Officer Perez had to hold him with both hands to keep him from falling.

Is this what it was like for Dad? Will thought as the room spun around him. *Did he feel like this when they threw him in a cell when he didn't even do anything wrong?*

"Sit in this chair, kid," Officer Perez said.

Will sank into a seat he couldn't see, and the policeman pushed Will's head between his knees. The room stopped spinning. Will felt like a damp dish towel.

The door opened again, and he heard his mother give a startled cry.

"He's okay," Officer Perez said. "He just got a little light-headed."

"Get me a cold cloth," Mom said. "And make it snappy."

Above Will's head there was a pause, and then he heard retreating footsteps. Mom squatted beside him, her cool hand on the back of his neck.

"You all right, Son?" she said.

"No," Will said. His voice couldn't get around the lump, so it broke. "I don't wanna go to jail. I can't handle it either, just like Dad. I can't go in some cell—"

"You're not going into a cell." It was Judge Kohn's voice, commanding but calm. Will pulled out from under his mother's hand and looked up at him.

"I said I would take you into my custody," the judge said, "and that's what I'm going to do. I'm going to personally take you to your home and see that you are properly placed, and then I will give explicit instructions to your keeper as to what you may and may not do."

"Officer Perez is gonna be my keeper?" Will said.

"No. Your mother is. You will not be allowed to leave the

premises until we get this cleared up. If you do, then I *will* have to make other arrangements."

"That won't be necessary," Mom said. "Right, Son?"

"Right!" Will said. This time it was his head that was spinning. He closed his eyes to stop it, and to keep the tears from escaping.

"Now, then," said the judge, "three things before we go. One—" He held up an important-looking finger. Will opened his eyes and watched it as if it were his last lifeline. "You'll give Officer Perez the names of the three boys you mentioned."

"Yes, sir," Will said.

"Two—you'll give us any information you can about Fawn's possible location. I have several officers on it at the moment, but I'll expect your cooperation."

"Yes, sir. But if you'd let me go look for her, I bet I'd find her right away."

Judge Kohn put his face close to Will's, and his bright blue eyes were pencil-sharp. "Hear me, Will," he said. "You are under house arrest. You leave that house and I'll know you can't be trusted. Am I clear?"

This time Will just nodded.

"We'll have a lot to talk about while you're 'locked up'," Mom said.

"Ah—which leads me to the third thing." The judge's eyes sharpened even more. "I am still expecting an article from you tomorrow—something about anti-Semitism, I believe?"

"I don't understand," Mom said. "This has nothing to do with Will's views of the Jews or anyone else. I haven't been the mother I should be and—"

"I'm just covering all the bases," the judge said.

God? Will wanted to yell. *I'm praying here! Who has the instructions?*

He looked at his mother, who was contemplating the top of his head and obviously planning the "talk" they were going to have when they got home. He looked at Judge Kohn. He was making notes on a notepad. The door opened, and he looked at Officer Perez who was bringing in a wet cloth. There were no instructions in any of them. There was only a thought, alone and clear in his head.

He pushed the cloth away and stood up. "It doesn't have anything to do with any of that!" he said. "I'm innocent and so is Fawn!"

"Will," Mom said. Her voice had that don't-fool-with-me edge to it. "Officer Perez saw that pin fall out of your pocket." She glanced at the policeman. "Why would he lie?"

"It *did* fall out of my pocket!" Will said. "I found it in the front yard this afternoon, and I put it in my pocket so I could ask Fawn about it, but then everything else happened and I didn't have a chance."

Mom studied his eyes. "Okay," she said slowly.

"We need to find your girl," said Judge Kohn. "She needs to be in my 'custody,' too—"

"But she didn't take it!" Will faced him squarely. "Luis and Rafael and Pablo did! They were in the store the first time Mr. Spitz accused Fawn of stealing, and just today she *saw* them take stuff from the Indian women at the Palace. She tried to follow them and she lost them so she went to Mr. Spitz's shop to see if they were there and that's why he saw her back there."

Mom looked confused. Judge Kohn didn't. His eyes bored into Will's. "That doesn't explain how the pin got on your front lawn. Are you suggesting those three young men planted it there, just to make you and Fawn look guilty?"

It did sound lame, even to Will. Every time he and Fawn had run into Luis and company, it had been accidental. It was never as if Luis and Rafael and Pablo followed them with a plan in mind. All Will could say was, "Maybe."

"Visit their homes," Judge Kohn said to Officer Perez. "Get names, everything, from the boy." He looked at Will. "This isn't a game, Son," he said. "You can't use this to get back at some boys who've given you a hard time."

"I'm not," Will said. "I'm just trying to follow instructions."

"Instructions?" Mom said. "Whose instructions?"

Will bit his lip.

"Whose instructions are you talking about?" Mom said.

"I can't help you if you don't tell me everything," the judge said.

That sounded like pretty clear direction to Will. He looked the judge square in the eye.

"God's instructions," he said. "That's what Pastor Bud told me to do, and that's what I'm doing. And I'm expecting it to help."

He also expected the judge to shake his head or bark that this crazy boy be locked up after all. To his surprise, Judge Kohn just rested a hand on his shoulder for a second. Then he said, "Let's get you home."

Nobody said much to Will in the car, which gave him a chance to think.

I gotta talk to Fawn. I gotta tell her that we're telling the truth—no more hiding. If she finds out from somebody else, she's gonna think I ratted on her. She's going to think I didn't protect her—like a brother.

They turned the corner onto Canyon Road just then, and Judge Kohn slowed the car and glanced at Mom.

"Who's that parked in front of your house?"

"I have no idea. I don't recognize the car."

Will did. It was a long, funny-looking vehicle with a front that looked like the back. What had Officer Perez called it—a Studebaker?

It was like the one he and Fawn saw cruising Canyon Road during every blackout.

It was like the one Mr. Spitz drove to the police station.

"What in the name of Moses?" Judge Kohn said.

He lurched his own car to a stop behind the Studebaker and shook his head as a stiff-moving figure with big ears leapt from its front seat, leaving the door gaping open.

"That's Mr. Spitz!" Mom said. "Does the man never give up?"

Evidently not, because he marched straight to Judge Kohn's window and proceeded to yell through the glass. The judge wound it down wearily, and Will slid down in the backseat.

But Mr. Spitz didn't even look in Will's direction. He spat all his words at Judge Kohn.

"What have they done with Abraham?" he cried.

"Abraham?" Judge Kohn said.

"Do you mean Abe?" Mom said.

"Where is my grandson? He's gone—where is he?"

Will forgot about hiding from the old man, because he could only stare at him. His eyes were wild behind his glasses, as if he were looking right at Judge Kohn but seeing the Devil himself. His forehead oozed sweat all the way up to the shock of hair in the front, which was now standing straight up as if it had been commanded to do so by the madman below.

"The idiot!" Mr. Spitz raved on. "He'll go off with anyone—even thieves! Where have you taken him?"

By now Mr. Spitz's eyes were on Mom, but they obviously weren't scaring her for a moment. She had already drawn herself up in the seat and was leaning across Judge Kohn to make herself heard.

"The poor kid has probably run away," she said. "And I can't say that I blame him. I only hope he's found a safe place to hide until the court can get him away from you!"

Judge Kohn reared his head back and shoved a hand through his thinning hair. "Ingrid," he said tightly. "Don't make this worse."

"It can't get any worse!" Mr. Spitz said.

"No, it can't!" Mom said over him.

"Enough!" the judge said—over *both* of them.

The car fell silent, except for Mr. Spitz's angry breathing. The judge looked from one of them to the other before he continued.

"I will notify the police that your grandson is missing," he said, "and he will be found. He is obviously not with the Hutchinsons because they are with me."

For the first time, Mr. Spitz's eyes landed on Will, and his mouth opened again for more spewing. The judge cut him off.

"Say another accusatory word, Mr. Spitz," he said, "and you'll have me to reckon with. Now go home. When we find your grandson, we'll let you know."

The judge then waited until Mr. Spitz finally stormed back to his Studebaker and roared off down Canyon Road.

"I ought to have them pick him up for reckless driving," the judge said. He sighed. "May I come in and use your phone, Ingrid?"

They all went into the house, and while Mom was showing the judge to the phone, Will raced upstairs. The attic was like an oven when he got there, but he barely noticed. A little more sweat on top of the drenching his fear had already given him tonight wasn't going to change much. With a clammy hand he pressed in on the secret panel and it gave obediently. Behind it, there was a moan.

Will stopped and peered into the dark compartment. "Fawn?" he said.

There was another moan. And then the mournful words, "Bad boy. Very, very bad boy."

✥ ✥ ✥

Chapter Eighteen

*A*be?" Will said.

He pushed the panel back farther and stuck in his hand. A big hand fumbled clumsily for his and clung to it.

"Abe—what are you doing here?" Will said.

There was no answer—just more moaning. Will pulled away, went to the chain that hung from the light bulb in the middle of the attic, and gave it a yank. It gave out a dusty sort of light, enough to reveal big Abe, stuffed into the secret compartment like a pickle in a jar, one hand pressed against his mouth in a fist, the other clutching something.

"Is Fawn in there with you?" Will said. He rolled his eyes. "Of course she's not. I'm surprised *you* fit in there." His mind groped around, looking for an explanation. "Did you come here when you got scared?"

Abe nodded.

"Well—that's good—and we're gonna protect you." Will almost grinned. He could already picture Mom throwing herself over Abe and shaking her fist at Mr. Spitz.

"So—when you came in—did Fawn come out?"

Abe looked puzzled and shook his head.

"Then how did you find this place?"

To his surprise, Abe's big face broke into a smile, all teeth. "Baby Abey!" he said. And then he began to gurgle on in German.

"Wait!" Will said. "English, Abe. Speak English!"

Will felt a little like the Sisters, but he didn't get the same result they did. Abe just looked confused for a second, and then held up the object he'd been clutching. Will peered at it in the dim light.

It was a pillow.

"*Kopfkissen*," Abe said. "Baby Abey."

It did indeed look like a baby's pillow. It was made of pale blue satin and had ribbons hanging from it. One of them looked browned and crumpled, as if a baby had chewed on it a long time ago and it had been left to dry.

"You brought your baby pillow—*kopfkissen*—with you?" Will said.

Abe shook his head and jabbed a thumb into the compartment.

"I don't get it," Will said. "But come on—tell it to Mom. She speaks a little German."

He reached in to take Abe by the wrist, but the big boy hung back, clutching the pillow to his chest.

"I'm not gonna take it away from you," Will said.

Bleating like an injured sheep, Abe thrust the pillow at him again. Gingerly, Will took it while Abe watched him carefully.

"Uh, nice pillow," Will said, for lack of anything else to say.

Abe gave a little whimper and kept watching.

"O-kay." Will looked at the pillow again. "It's pretty."

Abe nodded pensively.

"Uh—it's clean." It was, in fact, a little too clean for being carried around for fifteen years. All Will's old baby toys had long ago disintegrated. There was just a little dust on this, and that one dingy-looking ribbon.

Abe nodded again and pointed at the pillow.

"There's not much more to say about it, pal," Will said. "Oh, let's see—something's stitched on here—"

There was some embroidery in one corner that looked like initials. D. A. P.

"Must be the person that made it," Will said. "Your initials would be A. Something S.—Abraham Spitz."

"No Spitz!"

The words came out of Abe sounding like his grandfather's spewing. Will blinked at him.

"Oh," he said. "He must be your mother's father. So your last name's not Spitz."

Abe shook his head, so as to leave no doubt.

"I don't blame you. I wouldn't want that man's name either. What *is* your name? You told it to me that day at the school—at the Opportunity School—with Sister Miriam George, remember?"

"George!" Abe crowed happily.

"Yeah. Her name's Miriam George. What's yours?"

Abe's face grew serious with concentration. He formed the words on his lips first, then said them. "Abraham Fetzer."

"Oh." Will looked at the pillow. "A. F. That's not D. A. P. What am I doing?" Once again he reached for Abe. "It's a great pillow, Abe, but we got stuff to do. We gotta find out where Fawn is—we gotta see if they found any of your grandfather's stuff at Luis's—we gotta figure out how that pin ended up in our front yard—"

Will stopped. He wasn't sure where it came from, but there was suddenly a flash—a flicker of a memory in his head. He closed his eyes and tried to get it back.

A hand coming out a car window.

A car that was passing their house in the dark of a blackout.

A car that looked the same in the front as in the back.

A Studebaker—like Mr. Spitz drove.

"He's Fawn's spy!" Will cried. "He put it there—"

But why? Why would Mr. Spitz go to all that trouble to make Fawn and Will look guilty?

"Will?"

It was Mom, calling from the second floor. Abe gave a happy little cry, but then he grabbed his pillow from Will and shrank back into the compartment, fist to his mouth.

"It's okay, big fella," Will said. "She likes you. She's gonna protect you."

Either Abe didn't understand, or he wasn't buying it. He pulled back farther. Will searched his memory.

"She's like a *mutter*," Will said.

That did it. Abe scrambled out of the compartment, still clutching the pillow, and went straight for the attic door.

"Will?" Mom called again.

"Mutter?" Abe answered her.

There was a bewildered silence below, which got deeper when Will shoved Abe in front of her on the landing.

"What on *earth?*" Mom said.

"I guess he came back here when his grandfather followed me and Officer Perez to the police station," Will said. "Fawn must have shown him the special hiding place before she took off."

"No," Abe said happily. "Baby Abey!" He gurgled out some German while Mom frowned to understand.

"What's he saying?" Will said.

"I get the words but I don't know what they mean," Mom said. "Something about he found the pillow in Baby Abey's place to hide if the bad people come." Mom twisted her mouth. "His grandfather definitely fits *that* category."

"Where's Judge Kohn?" Will said.

"He's downstairs talking to Officer Perez. That's why I was looking for you."

Will's mouth got dry as he hurried down the stairs. His stomach turned over when he saw the judge's face. He was perched at the edge of the window seat, hands between his knees, looking up at Officer Perez. His expression wasn't happy.

"Nothing?" the judge said. "You found nothing?"

"No Fawn?" Mom said.

"No," said the judge. "No Indian jewelry—not in any of the three boys' rooms, or in their clothes—"

"If you can call them clothes," Officer Perez said. "I never saw such a bunch of rags. I'm gonna go through my sister's kids' stuff tomorrow and see if I can't find some hand-me-downs they can have."

Will sank heavily to the window seat beside Judge Kohn. The hope was slowly draining out of him. *Pray. Expect. Follow instructions.*

What instructions, God?

"That still doesn't prove they didn't do it," Officer Perez said. "I'd like to bring the kids in, just to scare 'em a little. They might talk."

Will tried to picture Officer Perez shoving Pab the Stab and Louie the Luck and Raf the Rough into a cell in their zoot suits—

He sat up straight on the window seat, jiggling the judge's elbow. "Did you say *all* their clothes were ragged?" Will said.

"My wife uses better to dust the furniture," Officer Perez said.

"What about their zoot suits? They're practically brand-new."

"Zoot suits?" Mom said.

"Those things the young people have been wearing for swing dancing," Officer Perez said. "Some kind of statement of rebellion or something. Is that what you're talking about, Son?"

"Yes, sir," Will said.

Officer Perez fingered his moustache. "I didn't see anything like that."

"They weren't wearing them?" Will said.

"I don't know," said Officer Perez. "I didn't see the boys. Their parents didn't know where they were."

"At this time of night?" Mom said. And then she put her hand up to her lips. "I should talk. I don't know where one of mine is either."

I know where she is, Will thought. *She's out there hunting down Luis—and for nothing! It's Mr. Spitz we oughta be tracking down—*

But his shoulders sagged. That would be for nothing, too. Who was going to believe that Mr. Spitz had deliberately set it up to look like Fawn and Will were thieves? They couldn't prove that either.

And this time, no instructions came from God.

"Well," Judge Kohn said with a sigh, "at least one parent's gonna know where his kid is. I'd better call Spitz."

"You're not going to let him take this boy!" Mom said, eyebrows springing to life.

"What choice do I have, Ingrid?" the judge said. "Spitz hasn't done anything to the boy—"

"Except call him a stupid idiot and make him cower in corners!"

"Unfortunately there's no law against that," Judge Kohn said. "I've fudged enough for one night. I'll call him and let him know Officer Perez is on his way with him."

"At least make him come get him himself," Mom said. "I made the mistake of dropping Abe in front of the shop once, having no idea what was going to go on between the two of them. I won't do that again. I want to see this reunion."

"Fair enough," said the judge, and he went for the phone.

Abe had obviously understood some of the conversation, because he had already taken to moaning against his fist. Mom stroked his hair. Will could feel himself wilting.

Now she'll probably go back to making Spam and staring at the wall, he thought miserably. Just then, a miracle, even a small one, would have been nice.

None occurred before the doorbell rang and Mom let Mr. Spitz in. The old man ransacked the room with his eyes until they landed on Abe. Yet even as he started to storm toward his grandson, he stopped. Once again his eyes swept the living room, this time slowly, as if he hated everything in it.

"I looked around, Spitz," Judge Kohn said. "There's none of your jewelry here."

Mr. Spitz blinked abruptly and stirred himself back to Abe. He already had his finger pointed at Abe's nose when he noticed Officer Perez in the group, and once again he stopped.

"Well?" he said to the officer. "Did you search their homes? Did you find my jewelry?"

"No—"

"Of course you didn't, because they didn't do it—this one did!"

He whirled toward Will and for the third time that night, grabbed his shirt front and jerked him up.

"Get your hands off my son!" Mom cried.

"Spitz—don't be a fool!" the judge joined in. "Perez!"

Officer Perez folded his arms neatly around Mr. Spitz from behind and pulled him back. He dropped Will in a sputtering rage.

"Are you *completely* off your rocker?" Mom said to him. This time she was the one to whirl, on Judge Kohn, like an angry goose. "You aren't going to let *any* child go home with this man, are you?"

"He's my grandson!" Mr. Spitz cried. "You've taken everything else from me. You can't take him, too!" He shot out a hand and curled it around the front of Abe's shirt. "Abraham—come! We go back to that hovel they call our home!"

"No!"

The room looked like a hall of statues as everyone froze—except Abe.

"No!" Abe said again. "Home!"

He stomped his foot so hard the pottery jiggled on the mantel, and then before anyone could stop him, Abe shoved his grandfather aside and ran—through the dining room—into the kitchen—where they could hear him moaning. Will could practically see him rocking, fist in mouth.

Mr. Spitz started after him, but with a nod from Judge Kohn, Officer Perez held him back. He went into a rage in German.

"Judge, you cannot let him take this boy!" Mom said. "Listen to him in there—he's terrified!"

"We'll get this sorted out, Ingrid."

"At least let Will go to him. It'll calm him down."

Judge Kohn nodded, and Will was off like a flash. He found Abe crouched by the back screen door, sobbing.

"Come on, big fella, it's gonna be all right," Will said, but the thoughts began to do battle in his head.

Not that I believe that myself, one said.

But I have to, said another. *I have to keep expecting. I have to keep listening. I have to listen until I find a way.*

But there aren't any answers in this house. All they're doing is yelling in there. God, where are my instructions?

There was no other thought to answer that. Until a shadow appeared on the back screen door.

"Will?" a voice whispered.

"Fawn?"

"Shh!"

Will crawled from Abe to the door. Fawn was on the other side.

"We got real trouble," he whispered to her.

"I know. I've been listening."

"Where were you?"

"Under the back steps."

"All this time? Never mind. You gotta go out again. You gotta find out some stuff."

"Not by myself."

"Since when?"

"Since I got used to you being my brother. I'm scared, Will."

Will pressed his nose against the screen to see her better. There were tears sparkling in her good eye. The other one was already turning black and blue. Beside him, Abe was moaning. In the living room, the adults were screaming. Judge Kohn had said if he left here, he would know Will couldn't be trusted and he would have to make other arrangements. Somehow that didn't sound like God's instructions. It didn't sound the way things sounded when they came out of Bud's mouth.

"Okay," Will said. "I got an idea."

"What? Anything—I'll do anything—"

"Then come on. We're going to Bud's."

He inched the screen door open. Abe gave a soft gasp.

"Well, come on, big fella," Will said. "You're coming with us."

And while the battle raged on in the living room, Will and Abe slipped out with Fawn and were gone.

✝ ✦ ✝

Chapter Nineteen

*A*lthough the New Mexico night was windy, Will was sweating by the time they'd skirted Santa Fe and were peeking out from behind the garage in Bud's backyard. The wind was rolling a storm down from the Jemez Mountains and across the valley, and it had Abe trembling against Will and Fawn.

"Would you get this big oaf off of me," Fawn said.

"Big idiot," Abe mumbled.

"Whatever he is, does he have to lean on me?"

"He's scared. We all are," Will said. "And Bud's gonna help us."

"How do you know he's not gonna just take us back home?" Fawn said.

"I don't. He might do that. But if he says we have to, then we'll know it's what we're supposed to do."

"Why?"

"Because he always gets his instructions from God."

"What?"

"Would you just—just trust me, okay?"

"You're getting weird, Will," she said.

The sky flickered with lightning. Abe gave a yelp and buried his face in Fawn's back. She glared at Will, but in the flash he could see her eyes were frightened.

"Come on," he said.

Through the living room window, they could see Bud and Tina in their chairs. There was a soft light coming from a lamp between them. Bud was reading the paper; Tina was mending a sock. The radio was on. It looked so peaceful and inviting, Will wanted to cry.

Another fork of lighting stabbed through the sky, and Bud frowned at the radio. He leaned over to adjust it, and his eye caught their movement at the window. Will saw his Elmer Fudd face spring to life.

He said something to Tina and hurried out the door. Tina kept mending.

"I thought you three might show up," he whispered to them as he met them in the bushes. "Your mother just called. Fawn, that's quite a shiner you've got there."

Will's heart fell and so, apparently, did his face, because Bud put a hand on his shoulder.

"You've been listening for instructions?"

"Yeah—and I thought I was getting them, but—"

"I've gotten a few of my own." His eyes went to Abe. "Hey, there," he said. "I'm Pastor Bud. I'm a friend."

Abe didn't even flinch. His face broke into a grin, and he stuck out a hand to shake Bud's. Will was expecting the hug any minute.

"I have somebody else I want you to meet," Bud said. "Why don't you come on inside with me?"

Although Will could feel his eyes springing open with alarm, Abe apparently saw no reason not to follow Bud right into the house. Will and Fawn watched through the window as the handshaking commenced with Tina, and Abe trailed her into the kitchen. Bud picked up the phone.

"What's he doing that for?" Fawn said.

"I don't know," Will said. But his heart was picking up speed again, and a little hope was seeping back in.

They watched Bud talk into the receiver, hang up, and go out the front door. "Psst, over here!" he hissed to them from the front walk.

Will crept out, and Fawn followed reluctantly, hugging herself against the wind.

"Abe was going to slow us down," Bud said in a low voice. "Tina will take care of him. You know how she loves kids."

"Are you going to hide us?" Fawn said.

"No," Bud said, "I'm going to take you home."

Fawn turned on Will, fists already doubled, but Bud rested his hand over them.

"In one hour. I told your mother you were here and that I was going to feed you and pray with you and I'd bring you home in one hour. I've got to be true to my word."

"He's just gonna turn us in!" Fawn said to Will.

Will turned what he knew was a bewildered face to Bud.

"I can't go against the law," Bud said. "But my instructions tell me you could use an hour to straighten out the mess your mother told me about when she called me."

"What instructions?" Fawn said. She tossed back the hair that the wind was throwing into her face. "From who?"

"From Ingrid," Bud said. "She asked me to help you."

"She meant pray with us, I bet," Will said. "She still thinks we had something to do with all this—that we were just trying to get attention."

"I don't think she does," Bud said. "Otherwise, why would she have said, 'Give them whatever they need, Bud. That's what Rudy would do'?" He grinned his sloppy grin. "You want something for that eye, Slugger?"

Fawn shook her head.

"Then I think the first thing you need is a dry car to ride in, because here comes the rain."

It started to come down in its first big, angry drops, and the three of them ran through it to the garage where they piled into the front seat of Bud's old Chevy. Fawn was still looking doubtfully up at Bud, especially when the engine had an asthma attack before it would start. But Will's mind was clear of all doubt. He was getting instructions almost faster than he could get them out.

"All right," he said, sitting up straight and ignoring the spring in the seat that was poking him in the backside. "First, we gotta prove it was Mr. Spitz who was driving by our house all the time at night—because then they might believe he threw that pin out on our lawn."

"If he drove by every night, some of the other neighbors probably saw him, too," Bud said.

"It wasn't every night," Will said. "Mostly just during blackouts."

"Oh. That's interesting. It also makes it harder. You might have been the only people who noticed—"

"The air raid warden noticed him," Fawn said. "We heard him yelling through his bullhorn."

"Now you're talking," Bud said. "I think the warden's office is on Lincoln."

The rain was lashing against the windshield when they got to the office, which Bud said was a good thing because there wouldn't be many people out and about.

"Still," he said, "it wouldn't be a bad idea for you two to hunker down in here while I go in."

As soon as he was gone, Fawn said, "I wanna run."

"Why?"

"Because what good's this gonna do?"

"I don't know," Will said.

Fawn rearranged herself on the floor of the car and looked at him closely. "Now I'm really scared," she said. "You always know! You can always make me believe I'm wrong and you're right. You're so—realistic."

Will could only shrug. His stomach wasn't turning over. He didn't have a giant lump in his throat. He was still breathing, and his heart was still beating. It *felt* like this was the thing to do—and he could only believe that was part of following instructions.

"I don't think being realistic all the time is all that—realistic," he said.

"What does that mean?"

Will didn't have a chance to answer. The driver's side door flew open and Bud flung himself in, dripping rain from his very eyebrows.

"Good news!" he said. He was smiling so big, it was hard to tell what were the happy beads of spit and what were raindrops. "The warden said he did spot a car out on Canyon Road during the last blackout. What kind of car does Mr. Spitz drive?"

"Funny-looking," Fawn said.

"Studebaker," Will said.

"Bingo! That's what he saw—and with no license plate to trace it. Now—where do you suppose that Studebaker is right now?"

"Parked in front of my house, probably," Will said.

"Nope. Your mother said everybody had left. Next guess."

"At his shop—in the back."

"I'm not going there!" Fawn said.

"Why do we want his car, anyway?" Will said.

"If he tossed a pin in the yard from it, there might be more in the vehicle," Bud said. "However—" he glanced at his watch. "We have to use our time wisely."

"How much we got?"

"Forty-five minutes. The shop's on the other side of town. Where might he be in this direction, since we're over here? Where might he be looking for his grandson?"

"I've never seen him anyplace else," Will said. "Except the Plaza Restaurant."

"And the movies," Fawn said. "I saw him once at the Lensic, but he didn't stay for a whole show."

"Why would he go to the movies if Abe was missing, anyway?" Will said.

"You got me," Bud said. "But why would he go to a movie and not stay for the whole thing, either?"

"Because he's nuts," Fawn said.

"I'm beginning to believe that," Bud said. "Let's just cruise by the Lensic."

To their disappointment, there was no Studebaker parked any place close by the front of the castle-like theater when they got there.

"Where did he park before?" Bud said to Fawn.

"He didn't. He walked."

"All the way from his shop?" Bud said. "Spry old guy, isn't he?"

"No, he's just a cranky old—"

"Fawn," Will said sharply.

"Well, let's just take a gander at his shop, then," Bud said. "You two keep your eyes peeled while I drive—"

"Wait!" Will said.

Bud jammed on the brakes, and the Chevy slid sideways on the wet street. Will rubbed the fog off the inside of the window and peered out.

"What?" Fawn said. "Do you see him?"

"No—but I just saw something green—and blue—back there, Bud! Isn't there an alley on the side?"

"Yeah," Fawn said. "What did you see? Oh—zoot suits!"

"Go back in the alley, Bud!" Will said.

"You got it," Bud said, and he whipped the car into the alley.

Fawn latched onto Will's arm. "Why are we following them?"

"Instructions!" Will said.

Fawn rolled her eyes and hung on.

Bud shot through the alley like spit through a tin horn, but there appeared to be nothing in it but rain. A flash of lightning confirmed that. The Chevy reached the end where a back alley ran perpendicular, and Bud looked at Will. "You got two choices; left or right?"

Fawn leaned one way, Will the other. He saw a blur of green.

"That way!" he said. "Go that way!"

"But he'll see the car and get away!" Fawn said.

"You two mind getting wet?" Bud said.

Nobody had to answer. The car doors were pried open and all three of them sprinted out into the rain. Will peered through and caught his blur of green. So did Fawn.

"I got Rafael!" she hissed, and she took off after him.

"Do we have a blue one?" Bud said.

"That's Pablo!"

"I'm on him. You take the brown fella."

"What brown fella?"

But he needn't have asked. He had only to turn around to watch Bud go, and Luis was suddenly in front of him, as if he had dropped from the sky with the storm.

In reality he'd probably only come from the fire escape—and he was ready for a fight. His eyes gleamed meanly, and his mouth was held like a gash across his face.

Will forced himself to plant his feet in a confident stance.

"I don't wanna fight," Will said. "I just wanna know something."

"Too bad, An-glow," Luis said out of his gash of a mouth. " 'Cause I don't know nothin'."

Luis pulled back his arm, fist doubled. Will bent his head and dove straight for his chest. Caught by surprise, Luis slid backward on the wet bricks with Will on top of him. They both slapped to the ground, the zoot suit opening out like a sail as they went.

When they finally landed, Will kept his head down to avoid any punch Luis might manage to throw. But he forgot about fists and fights and everything else as he took in what was right next to his face.

The zoot coat lay open, and inside it, fastened in neat rows as if they were on display, were enough decorative pins and necklaces and bracelets of turquoise and silver to start an Indian jewelry store. Will whipped his head to the other side of the coat. Both sides were filled, and not with the imitation trinkets Mr. Spitz sold in his shop. This was the real stuff, just like the Indian women showed in front of the Palace.

Luis wasn't going to give Will a chance to look much closer. He raised both arms and with the heels of his hands shoved Will backwards. Will rolled over and tried to crawl away, but Luis was on him at once, flattening him to the ground. His lip hit the bricks and there was a sharp pain as his front teeth chomped down. The metallic taste of blood filled his mouth.

Will tried to bump Luis off of him, but the wiry Hispanic boy was already at work, wrenching both of Will's arms behind his back. Will was sure he was going to be folded into a back bend, and that was a hold he couldn't budge from—

Until Luis gave a startled cry and Will was suddenly free. Will rolled over to the sound of a scuffle behind him. He sat up to see Fawn trouncing Luis into submission, his back flat on the bricks.

"That'll teach you to ever jump my brother again!" she said.

"Pablo!" Luis shouted. "Rafael!"

Will looked frantically around him, but Fawn only snickered.

"Don't bother," she said. "They're already tied up."

"Where?" Will said. He was on his feet by now and grabbing Luis around the ankles so he wouldn't kick Fawn, who was sitting astride him as if he were a calf she'd just easily roped.

"In the backseat of Pastor Bud's car," she said. "He's got just enough rope left to tie this one up."

"No one ties me!" Luis cried.

Will was sure he was probably right, but Pastor Bud himself appeared just then, grinning his sloppy grin and carrying a piece of thick rope.

"I always carry plenty of towing rope," he said to Will as he got to his knees in the rain and proceeded to tie it around Luis's body and arms while Fawn sat on his legs. "You have to when you drive a jalopy like mine." He gave Will a closer look. "I guess I'd better start carrying a first aid kit if I'm going to pal around with you two. Is that as bad as it looks?"

Will wiped his mouth on his arm and shook his head.

"Then we'd better get this one in the car," Bud said.

Luis didn't go quietly. All the way to the car, he wriggled like a caught flounder and yelled things in Spanish Will was glad he didn't understand. But they got him there and tossed him into the backseat where Pablo and Rafael were already propped up in their own ropes like a pair of mummies. Their mouths weren't covered, but once Bud started the car and started to ask questions, they clamped them shut and would only stare at the backs of Will and Fawn's heads. Nobody, obviously, was doing any poking now.

"You want to tell us where you got all that nice jewelry?" Bud said. "Before we get to the police station?"

Apparently not.

"You don't want to tell us the story, in case we can help you out?"

Definitely not.

"I don't want to help them anyway," Fawn muttered to Will.

But Will didn't answer. As they turned the corner from San Francisco Street, something caught his eye that made him shout, "Bud! Stop!"

Bud did, and they all rocked forward. The three boys in the back tumbled against each other like loose milk bottles in a crate. The three in the front stared through the windshield at the car parked in front of St. Francis Cathedral.

It was Mr. Spitz's Studebaker.

✝ ✝ ✝

Chapter Twenty

F awn was the first to come to life.

"Isn't that old man Spitz's car?" she said.

"Yeah!" Will said.

"Isn't he Jewish?" Bud said.

"Uh-huh."

Bud chuckled. "This is an odd place for him, then."

"He's probably looking for Abe at the school," Will said. "Except—it's not open this time of night."

"He's nuts," Fawn said.

"I think we ought to take advantage of this opportunity," Bud said, "as long as we're here."

"You mean look in his car?" Will said.

Bud nodded. "You've got us to keep watch. I'll flash the headlights if we see him coming. Don't touch or take anything—just have a look."

Will felt a chill, partly from his rain-soaked clothes and partly from the thought of Mr. Spitz catching him poking around in his Studebaker. But the instructions were coming thick and fast now, and there didn't seem to be any choice but to follow them. He opened the door and got out. At least it had stopped raining—

But his thoughts collided with what he saw in the backseat as he closed the Chevy door. It was the expressions on the faces of the three boys in the backseat. Pablo and Rafael were both looking at Luis as if they were about to throw up and wet their pants, respectively. And the look in Luis's eyes was one Will had never seen there before. It was the look of sheer terror.

"You better step on it, pal," Bud said. "We only have about 15 minutes of our hour left."

Will nodded and hurried off through the shadows of the cotton-woods to the Studebaker parked at the curb. He'd think about what was suddenly going on with Luis and company later. Right now he had to find some evidence in Mr. Spitz's car. He had to.

It was that same feeling, that feeling of *having to*—for Fawn and for himself and for Abe and even for Mom—that stopped his hands from shaking enough to open the car door and that kept his eyes from going into panicked blinking as he swept them around the interior.

He didn't see anything, not even a stray jacket or a candy bar wrapper or any of the things a person could have found in Mom's Hudson at one time. Will glanced up, but the headlights on the Chevy weren't flashing. He wiped his sweating palms on his pants and climbed inside.

I don't even like being in that nasty man's car, he thought. *Just thinking about him sitting in this seat gives me the creeps.*

Will even shuddered as he ran his hand under it. Just one little pin, that's all he needed to find. But his hand didn't hit anything except what felt like a leather satchel. Glancing up one more time to make sure Bud wasn't signaling him, Will pulled the bag out and unbuckled it. What he saw made him gasp.

The inside of the bag looked like the inside of Luis's zoot jacket. It was filled with handmade Indian jewelry.

I don't get it, he thought. *Mr. Spitz doesn't sell this stuff in his store. Why's he buying it?*

But of course, Will knew at once, he wasn't buying it. Luis and his friends were stealing it for him.

Will didn't have to remind himself of Bud's warning not to touch or take anything. He was happy to buckle the bag back up and shove it under the seat. He was even happier to scramble out of the car and close the door behind him. He was about to run back to the Chevy when he heard something.

The noise came from the other direction, and it was enough to stop him in his tracks to listen.

"Mr. Spitz, I have told you, we have not seen Abe since this afternoon—"

"I know that. Just open the building and I will find him!"

"But he couldn't possibly be—"

"Open the door!"

There was a shriek of "Mercy" that stopped Will's heart. That shriek was Sister Miriam George. The other voice was Sister Mary Harold.

"That was completely uncalled for, sir. You'll get nowhere with your threats!"

"Will I get somewhere with *this?*"

It was Mr. Spitz's voice, undoubtedly, and from the cry of "Mercy! Mercy!" Will could imagine what the "this" was. Picturing the old man snatching up Sister Miriam George by the front of her habit and shaking her until her face popped from her wimple, Will tore down the walk beside the cathedral and slid into the shadow of one of the Romanesque columns. From there he could see Mr. Spitz holding Sister Miriam George in front of him as he walked with his hand over her mouth, and Sister Mary Harold hurrying ahead, fumbling with her keys. They were headed for the Opportunity School.

Will hesitated in the shadows. *What should I do?* he thought frantically. *Maybe I oughta go get Bud. Maybe he should go get the police—*

He set one foot out of the shadow of the column, pointed toward the front of the cathedral, but before he could move the other one,

Mr. Spitz shouted, "Hurry up!" A muffled cry came from Sister Miriam George. Sister Mary Harold said, "I'm hurrying, Mr. Spitz—please—patience," in a voice edged with alarm.

Will turned toward the school and, crouching down from the waist, ran in and out of the shadows to reach the door to the chicken house just as it closed behind Mr. Spitz and the Sisters.

Will crept to it and peered through the indented window. Sister Miriam George was against one wall, crying into her hand. Sister Mary Harold planted herself in front of her friend and watched through her glasses, their chains quivering, as Mr. Spitz pierced himself into one part of the room and then another like an angry arrow.

"I told you he couldn't possibly be here," Sister Mary Harold said. "You saw how I had to unlock the door—"

"Quiet!" Mr. Spitz said, aiming himself at her. "We go into another building."

"I hardly think there's any point—"

"We go!" Mr. Spitz cried, and he grabbed Sister Miriam George by the arm and shook her like a weapon at Sister Mary Harold.

The tall Sister hurried to the back door of the chicken house and opened it to let Mr. Spitz and his hostage out. When the door closed behind them, Will left the window and tore around the side of the chicken house. He got to the back in time to see them disappear into the adobe stable. When a look through the window assured him they had gone into the next room, he let himself soundlessly in the door and hid behind the puppet theater. He could hear their voices—

"What is all this?" Mr. Spitz was saying. "No wonder my grandson shows no sign of becoming a man. You have him sewing pillows like a woman!"

"It strikes me as odd, Mr. Spitz," Sister Mary Harold said, "that you are showing this sudden interest in Abraham. This is the first time you have been to this school since you enrolled him."

"That makes no difference now! I am taking him tonight to Albuquerque. They have a place for him there, a place where he belongs."

"What kind of place?"

"An institution. He is an idiot and he cannot be trusted. He must be locked up!"

The suggestion shook through Will and right out through his hands. They jerked, and the front of the puppet theater wavered and began a forward fall. Will dove for it and caught it—but not before it clattered against the set of shelves that held the puppets. Papier-mâché figures fell against each other like dominos until the one at the end toppled off. To Will's horror, it landed right on top of the head that poked itself through the door. Mr. Spitz's blazing eyes found Will.

"You!" he shouted.

His long face went purple as he lunged for Will. Every nerve was shot through with fear as Will ducked. He landed on a papier-mâché burro and felt it smash under his weight. He reached beneath him, grabbed it, and flung it at Mr. Spitz. It grazed his cheek, but it didn't stop his coming straight at Will, his arms extended, his hands already formed to go around Will's throat.

"No!" Will screamed. "Get away from me!"

He flung himself backward, knocking over still another section of the puppet theater. Will caught his balance and twisted around to run. Mr. Spitz snagged him by the back of his shirt and shoved him, nose first, against the wall. More puppets bounced around them, but they went unnoticed by the angry man as he jerked Will to face him. His breath was so hot it stung Will's eyes.

"You will not have what belongs to me!" Mr. Spitz said. His teeth were gritted like a yellowed vice, yet still his words spit out in spurts. Will pulled his head as far out of reach as he could. That was how he saw what he saw. That was how he knew that someone else was listening to God's instructions.

"I have lost it all because I am a Jew!" Mr. Spitz said. "I have lost my daughter and then my wife and then—"

Will didn't find out what else Mr. Spitz had lost. From behind, a pillow was smashed over the old man's face, hard enough to knock him off balance. He careened backwards, into an avalanche of some 25 more cushions, poured down on him by Sister Miriam George.

"Sit on him, William," said a commanding voice.

Sister Mary Harold joined them with a familiar rope. It didn't take much effort for Will to plop himself down on top of Spitz and the pillows. He was already wobbly with sudden relief.

Sister Mary Harold reached under the screaming pile and came out with a wrist which she wrapped up in the rope.

"Hold this, Sister," she said to Sister Miriam George.

Sister Miriam took it as if it were a rattlesnake while Sister Mary Harold grabbed the other wrist, connected it to the first one, and dragged Mr. Spitz out from under the load of pillows. His face was magenta, and he was bawling out German. For the second time that night, Will was glad he didn't understand a foreign language.

Sister Mary Harold had Mr. Spitz's wrists tied to the iron leg of a worktable and was working on his legs when Officer Perez threw open the door, his gun already drawn.

"There will be none of that here, Officer," Sister Mary Harold said. "You can put that away."

Officer Perez obediently stuck the pistol back into its holster as he and the three other policemen behind him hurried over to the still-writhing, spewing Mr. Spitz. Bud stood just inside the doorway and held out an arm to Will. He ran to it without hesitation and flattened himself against Bud's spongy side. It might have been pudgy, but it felt as safe as any armored car could have.

"What happened in here?" Officer Perez said, looking around at the smashed puppets and their splintered theater.

"Just a bit of a tussle," Sister Mary Harold said. She was by now standing with her arm around the shoulders of a sobbing Sister Miriam George. "William was holding his own with Mr. Spitz here."

"Will—are you all right?"

It was Mom, rushing through the door just ahead of Judge Kohn. Her face was solid white, and her eyes nearly started from her head when they saw his mouth.

"That monster made you bleed!" she said.

"Nah, that wasn't him," Will said. "That's from—"

"I? I am the monster?" Mr. Spitz shouted. He struggled to wrench himself free from the four officers, but they held on as if they were restraining a rag doll. That, however, didn't stop the attack from his mouth. "You call me a monster? You are the monster, *Fraulein* Hutchinson! You take from one of your own kind what is mine—rightfully mine!"

"What are you bawling about, Spitz?" Judge Kohn said. "This woman hasn't taken a thing from you—"

"Look in their yard! Right in their front yard! You will find my merchandise there—"

Whether Mr. Spitz would have realized what he had just done, Will didn't have the chance to find out. Officer Perez nodded to his companions, who dragged Mr. Spitz to his feet and hauled him, still spewing English and German and spit, out of the building.

"Well now, Will," Judge Kohn said when they were gone. "It looks like I owe you an apology. Mr. Spitz just gave us the piece we needed to clear you, didn't he?"

"You said you found that pin in the front yard," Mom said, "and now we know how it got there."

"I even saw him throw it there during the blackout," Will said. "Only, I didn't think anybody would believe me."

Mom squeezed his shoulders with one arm. "We all had our opinions about why you did something you didn't do, that's for sure."

Will leaned around her to look at Bud, who was grinning sloppily at them from the corner. "Bud didn't," he said. "He knew."

"Just following instructions," Bud said.

✝ ⬧ ✝

Chapter Twenty-one

*T*he next day Will wanted to sleep until noon, but Mom dragged both him and Fawn out of bed early, and when they found out why, they were dressed and wolfing down cornflakes before she could get her hair up in its braid.

"Bud is going to take us over to the courthouse," she said. "Judge Kohn is going to see Luis and Pablo and Rafael in his chambers, and I personally want to find out what happens." She gave them both a sideways look. "I thought you two might be a little interested, too. Although you're a sight to take out anywhere, both of you—one with a black eye and one with a fat lip."

And then she did something that made Will grin, bigger and wider than he'd done all summer. She let the corners of her mouth twitch. It was like getting a present.

Bud and Mom and Will and Fawn sat on a bench in the hallway outside Judge Kohn's chambers. It wasn't the stern marble sanctuary Will had imagined. It was stucco and tile just like most buildings in Santa Fe—but still, there was a serious air about it. This was a place where decisions were made about people in deep trouble.

"It coulda been us," Will said, half to himself.

"Not a chance," Bud said. "You're listening now. The truth always comes out when you listen."

The door opened just then, and two big men in uniforms came out with three very small figures between them. It took Will a second glance to realize it was Pablo, Rafael, and Luis. They looked tiny and young in plain gray—without their zoot suits, and without their confident sneers. Pablo and Rafael stared miserably at the ground as they passed. Luis kept his eyes straight ahead—but they were no longer in mean little slits.

"He looks scared out of his mind," Fawn whispered to Will.

"Yeah," Will whispered back.

He was still staring after them in surprise as they disappeared down the hall and around a corner when the door opened again and Judge Kohn appeared. He was wearing a long black robe and Will realized the image he'd had of him once, looking down sternly from his bench, had been close to the truth. Even the lines in his face seemed deeper than usual.

"I heard you were all here," he said. "Why don't you come in?"

"No, thanks," Fawn said. "I think I'll just wait out here."

She was *still* staring after Luis and the boys and their guards, and her full lips were sucked in with concern.

"No, you'll need to come in," Judge Kohn said. "We still have a few pieces of this to sort out, and they concern you in particular, little one."

Will practically had to haul Fawn into the sunny chambers with its plain pine desk and clutter of papers. It didn't feel threatening anymore—but Fawn wasn't convinced of that. She sat on the edge of her chair as if to make sudden flight easier.

"The boys were quite cooperative," the judge said when they were settled. "They admitted that they have been working for Benjamin Spitz, stealing goods from the Indians in front of the Palace and giving them to him in return for certain things he promised them. The only thing he ever actually came through with was the zoot suits.

They never got the motorcycle, the radio, the unlimited chocolate bars."

That's why they looked so scared last night in the car, Will thought.

"He promised them all that?" Mom said. "Does the man have no conscience?"

"None whatsoever," Judge Kohn said. "Officer Perez tells me they still haven't gotten Mr Spitz to admit to anything."

Fawn stirred in her chair and poked Will. He cleared his throat.

"What about Fawn?" Will said. "Did Luis confess that they stuck that doll and that pin in Fawn's pockets the first day we were in his shop?"

Judge Kohn shook his head. "No, and I believe them. They said they followed you in there to give you a hard time, but Mr. Spitz scared them off—since they themselves had taken things from him before and had never been caught. Later he looked them up and asked them if they wanted to work for him, in exchange for the goodies and for him not making them pay for the damages done that day."

Fawn scooted even further to the edge of her seat until she was nearly falling off. Will saw her dart her eyes toward the door.

"Hideous," Mom was saying. "What's going to be done about Mr. Spitz?"

"He'll be prosecuted," Judge Kohn said. "He's being brought in for arraignment shortly. He's not the one I'm concerned about, though. I'm wondering what's to be done with young Abe." He looked at Bud. "Is he still with your wife?"

"They should be here any minute," Bud said.

Will remembered something and sat up straight. "You aren't going to put him in an institution, are you?" he said. "That's what Mr. Spitz wants to do with him—but that's not right. He's not crazy—"

"Let's just go out and see him, shall we?" the judge said. "These chambers might be intimidating to him, poor guy."

"What does 'intimidating' mean?" Fawn said to Will as they filed out.

"Makes you feel scared, like somebody's going to do something to you."

"Well, I'm still intimi—I'm still that."

God? Will thought. *We still need more instructions here. This isn't over yet.*

And it most certainly wasn't. As if by some evil plan, Tina and Abe appeared at one end of the hall just as two guards led a handcuffed Mr. Spitz in from the other end. Abe saw Will and broke away from Tina to run to him, arms open as wide as his smiling mouth. At that moment, Mr. Spitz looked up. He too tried to break away.

"Abraham!" he shouted. "Get away from those people! They are thieves! *Diebe!*"

Abe froze with his arms ready to go around Will. The smile left his face, and fright replaced it. He took a step away from Will and looked around in bewilderment. His hand went toward his mouth.

But Will reached up and grabbed it.

"You don't have to be afraid of him anymore, Abe," Will said. "We're your friends. *Freunds von mir.*"

Abe studied Will's lips as if he could still see the words there. Slowly, he looked up at his grandfather and, slowly, shook his head. Then he began to talk.

The words were in German, but they didn't fly out in uncontrolled fear. He spoke calmly, as if he were following instructions.

"What the devil is he saying?" Judge Kohn said.

"Oh, my," Mom said.

"What?"

She turned to them, eyes wide. "He says his grandfather is the thief. He put the pin in Fawn's pocket himself that day. Abe was in the back room watching."

"He is a liar!" Mr. Spitz cried. "You can't believe him—he is a stupid idiot—anyone can see that! He belongs in an institution!"

"You have to believe him, Mama Hutchie!" Fawn said. Her face twisted up. "Please believe him—don't send me away!"

Mom blinked. "Send you away? What are you talking about, Fawn? I never even considered sending you away, even if you'd stolen a car, for Pete's sake! I love you, no matter what."

Fawn couldn't answer. She was using up all her energy to hold back tears. Mom reached out one arm and scooped her into it, and scooped Will in with the other. His head stuck out over it, and he felt a little silly—for about a second. Then it just felt safe to be held by his mom, with his sister, with all the doubt wiped away.

Abe, however, didn't look safe. He stood watching the guards drag his grandfather into the courtroom, and he mouthed silently, "Idiot. Stupid idiot."

Will wished Mom had another hand to reach out to him. But her arms were full. Will was about to pull away and give Abe his place when someone else stepped forward and put her hand on Abe's sleeve.

"Don't you believe a word of it, Abe," Tina said. "You remember what I told you last night: You have everything God wanted you to have."

Abe looked down at her, his face a mask of questions.

"You have everything God wanted you to have," Tina said. "Except cherry lemonade. We need some of that right now."

Abe nodded, and slowly the smile spread over his face, farther than Will had ever seen it go before. Tina put her hand up and patted the back of Abe's neck. Bud smoothed Abe's back with his palm.

"Reverend Kates," Judge Kohn said, "have you and your wife ever thought about becoming foster parents?"

————

The very last of the pieces of their summer puzzle was put in place a week later when Judge Kohn came by to tell them that Mr. Spitz claimed that the Hutchinsons' house—was his.

"Why on earth would he think a thing like that?" Mom said.

"Because he's nuts," Fawn said.

"Fawn," Mom said.

"He's certainly disturbed," Judge Kohn said. "But a Joanna Pfetzer did buy this house with her husband David. They both left it and when they didn't return, the house went back to the bank. That took years, and of course was all done legally."

"No wonder this house was so familiar to Abe," Mom said.

Will felt himself frowning. "What's that got to do with Mr. Spitz?"

"Joanna Pfetzer was his daughter. He says she ran off to Germany looking for his 'stupid idiot' son-in-law who had gone looking for *his* brother and sister whom he feared had been picked up by the Nazis early on, long before the war. Joanna stopped getting letters from him and went to find him, leaving Abe with her parents. Neither Joanna nor David ever returned, and Mr. and Mrs. Spitz got word that they had probably been picked up by Hitler and taken to a camp. When the news started to leak out what those camps were about, Mr. Spitz's wife had a stroke and died and left him with Abe. He lost his senses and brought Abe here to try to get the house back. You were already living in it."

"So he tried to have my children put in jail?" Mom said. "Lord, forgive me, but he's worse than disturbed."

"At first he was just watching you," Judge Kohn said, "largely during blackouts when he thought he wouldn't be noticed. Meanwhile, he was building up another wave of hate, for the Indians."

"What did we ever do to him?" Fawn said indignantly.

"Your people created beautiful things that tourists and soldiers bought instead of buying his merchandise. When he tried to buy their things and resell them at a higher price, the Indians refused to sell to him. He decided it was because he was Jewish." The judge shook his head. "Interesting. He accused everyone else of being prejudiced against him because he was Jewish, and he turned right around and did the same thing to the Indians. When Fawn stumbled into his store that day, he saw a perfect opportunity to blame his streak of petty thievery on the people he hated. When he found out Fawn lived in this house, his need for vengeance just grew by leaps and bounds."

Mom frowned. "I know Abe is very happy right now, living with Tina and Bud, but I feel bad that he will never know anything of his mother and father except what his grandparents have told him—and I'm sure theirs was a pretty cockeyed version."

Will looked at Fawn, who was already looking at him.

"Maybe not, Mama Hutchie," Fawn said. "I think we've got just the thing for Abe."

And so the letters were pulled out of their hiding place, and that's when the final mystery was solved. Will studied the return addresses.

"I thought you said his last name was Fetzer," he said to Judge Kohn. "This name starts with a P."

"That's German for you," the judge said, chuckling. "The P is silent."

"So those are his initials on his pillow," Will said. "Except—D?"

"What's your name, Abe?" Fawn said.

Abe gave a wide grin. "David Abraham Pfetzer."

After that, Mom spent hours reading the letters to Abe. He seemed to love to hold them and smell them and even sleep with some of them under his initialed pillow over at Bud and Tina's in the special room they fixed up for him. Every day, his smile got bigger, until Will was *convinced* the boy had more teeth than any other human being on the face of the earth.

From then on, a summer that had crawled along as if it were dragging a burden behind it suddenly began to fly.

Abe showed Fawn and Will more secret places in the house. One they furnished with some of Abe's handmade pillows and hung out in to talk and tell jokes—because Abe would laugh at even the silliest ones—and munch on the marzipan Mom always had on hand.

In turn, Fawn and Will taught Abe how to find scrap metal and pull weeds in the Victory Garden and keep a scrapbook. His prized page was the one containing the picture of his mother he found in the box of letters. Will rolled his eyes when he saw Abe kissing it, but he secretly didn't blame him. A good mom was a nice thing to have.

And Will's was back. He knew it from the way Mom had all the women on Canyon Road rolling bandages for the Red Cross in her kitchen while they ate her now-famous strudel. He could tell from the fact that she volunteered to help the Sisters at the Opportunity School two afternoons a week, especially since there were all those puppets to remake.

One thing happened in late July that made Will afraid that she might slip back into her blues. They got a phone call from Uncle Al.

She barely gave Al a chance to talk at first, she was so busy apologizing for the way she had acted when he was with them. When he finally did get to the news he'd called with, all other thoughts were pushed aside. Fawn's father was receiving a medal.

"Silver Star," he said. "For bravery in the invasion of France. Fawn should be very proud of her daddy."

She was. Everybody knew by then that although the big operation was still going on, most of France had been recaptured from the Germans and they were retreating. For her father to be a hero in that would have given any daughter the grins, and Fawn definitely had them. She didn't stop smiling for days.

But Will kept watching his mother for signs of backsliding. After all, Rudy Hutchinson didn't have a chance to win medals. His reward for service to his country was a prison where he was probably treated worse than the rats that infested them. When he found Mom sitting in the window seat one hot afternoon, just staring out the window, Will got nervous enough to just ask her.

"Mom?" he said. "Are you gonna start hating everything again?"

She arched both eyebrows at him. "Why would I do that?"

"Because—of where Dad is?"

"You know something, Son?" she said, tucking her legs up under her thoughtfully. "I think we've all figured out that hating gets us absolutely nowhere. Look what it did to Mr. Spitz."

Will considered that. "And Luis and those guys," he said.

"Right. I see it all around us. A lot of people hate the mentally deficient and treat Abe like a dog. I got caught up hating the war, and it only put distance between you and me, between Fawn and me, even between your father and me. I completely stopped working for what I know is right."

"It was Abe who finally started changing your mind, huh?" Will said.

"Abe?" Mom said.

"Yeah. You started to perk up when I brought him over."

"No, Son, it wasn't Abe. It was you."

Will blinked.

"You showed so much compassion for him. You treated him like he was a human being. It was like God brought Abe into our lives so watching you with him could make me see what I was doing wrong."

"So I was your instructions from God?" Will said.

"I don't know what you mean," Mom said. But her eyes looked interested.

"Bud says if you pray and then expect God to answer and then look for the answers in everybody and everything, you'll get them."

"Does it work?"

"It does for me."

"Examples."

Will ticked them off on his fingers for her. Sister Mary Harold stopping him that night to tell him Mr. Spitz wasn't at home. Bud being on their side and giving them their hour. Fawn showing him that she needed him to be her brother. Just the feeling of having to do something—for all of them.

He stopped, because Mom's eyes were getting misty.

"Why are you crying, Mom?" he said.

"Me, cry?" she said. "You tell anybody and there will be no strudel for you for a week." Then she grabbed him around the head and held on. He let her for at least a minute before he wriggled away.

There was much to do the rest of the summer—have a Victory in France party, visit Judge Kohn's hacienda and swim in his pool, go on picnics at Camel Rock with Tina and Bud and Abe, go and see Abe's school puppet show. There was so much to do, in fact, that Fawn and Will had to give up the idea of their magazine. However, at the end of the summer Will did do his article for Judge Kohn. He took it to his chambers one day, and the secretary let him slip in between other appointments.

"My somber friend!" the judge said. "To what do I owe the honor?"

Will held out the article. "I don't have any money, so I hope you'll take this as payment."

The judge's bright blue eyes squinted. "Payment for what?" he said.

"I lost the bet. You know—you told me I couldn't get through the summer without seeing a miracle, and you won. I couldn't."

Judge Kohn sat back in his chair and folded his hands in the lap of his black robe. His eyes softened. "What miracle did you see?" he said.

"I saw a bunch."

"Do tell."

"Fawn believes my mom loves her. That's big. And my mom's back like she used to be. That's even bigger. And then there's Abe—he has parents again, and Bud and Tina have a kid, and that's what they always wanted."

The judge was nodding. "Is that what this article is about?"

"No," Will said. "It's the article you wanted. Only it turned out different. It's about how people get hate in them, especially against the Jews, when they don't even know them, and how it's gonna take a miracle to change that."

"You think it'll happen?" the judge said.

"Yes, sir," Will said.

"It will if you keep that attitude, Son." The judge sighed. "I wish there were more adults who think like you do. I might have my cousins right here with me now if they did. I'm afraid it's getting more hopeless by the day."

Will started to nod. After all, he was in a judge's chambers. But that didn't feel right, that nod. He just sat still.

The judge was watching him closely. "You don't agree?" he said.

"I have to believe that my dad's gonna live through prison camp and come home."

After a moment, the judge's bright blue eyes began to twinkle. "You know that could take a miracle," he said.

Will could feel his eyes twinkling back. "Don't you believe in miracles anymore?" he said.

"Should I?"

This time Will nodded without a second thought. After all, he had his instructions.

✟ ✟ ✟